From Participants of Lighthouse Writers Workshop's Community Engagement Programs

"I enjoy this workshop because it allows me to share a piece of myself that I feel others should know. Writing is a big form of therapy for me, and it helps me unload in a way that is private if I wish or in a way that is harmless to others. I journal daily and in a way, I hope that someday someone will read it and understand me better. My story left behind, so to speak. I think it benefits a lot of women here to tell their stories." —Julia V.

"I was so excited to hear that the Writing to Be Free program was going to hold workshops here in the facility. I'm a convicted felon and an adult mother whose family is torn apart from my drug use, bad behaviors and negative outlook on life. Just in the 1st class it has helped me to learn to write and open up about my feelings and that learn that I am not alone. I cried my eyes out, but for happiness this time. Thank you so much for bringing this workshop and these ladies & teachers into my life. I appreciate the experience." —Marilee L.

"This workshop is great and inspiring to me. It's something I've been looking for to express my thoughts & feelings for others to read. By having this workshop, I believe it will help others with life issues and to help them express themselves. For myself, I've always wanted to write & to become an author since childhood. This is perfect for me to get started, like a dream come true." —Dianna M.

"What does this workshop do for me? It lets me be me. It brings out this other side that I have not been able to explore about me. The way I can write now about how I feel and not be judged. This was my first class and I love it. I feel relaxed and excited when I get to share about what I wrote. These ladies were so inspirational and they are so positive and they listen, and that makes a big difference. I appreciate that we get to attend something like this."—Brenda C.

"This Writing to be Free workshop has helped me to break my writers block. After so many years of using, I found it hard to write upon becoming sober. This workshop not only has lovely instructors who are warm and inviting, but it provides a safe place for women to open up & share or simply listen & take in all the wonderful words of others. I thank you for providing such a freeing environment."—Jesse K.

All the Lives We Ever Lived

*A Lighthouse Writers Workshop
Community Anthology,
Volume 1*

Edited by Dan Manzanares & Suzi Q. Smith

And all the lives we ever lived
and all the lives to be
are full of trees
and changing leaves.

—Virginia Woolf, *To the Lighthouse*

Table of Contents

WRITING WITH CANCER WORKSHOP

HARD TIMES WRITING WORKSHOP— ARVADA PUBLIC LIBRARY

HARD TIMES WRITING WORKSHOP—
DENVER CENTRAL LIBRARY

THE GATHERING PLACE
WRITER'S GROUP

THE WRITE AGE—
DECKER PUBLIC LIBRARY

THE VETERANS AFFAIRS WORKSHOP

WRITING TO BE FREE

THE WRITE AGE—
GOLDEN PUBLIC LIBRARY

MICHAEL HENRY, EXECUTIVE DIRECTOR

Introduction

About three years ago, the Lighthouse staff made a careful decision to embark on community engagement programs for adults, something we'd wanted to do for years but didn't have the resources for. Our young writers' program had been running workshops in the community for years—in schools, detention centers, and elsewhere—so we knew the value of such work, and we wanted to expand the communities we served. Luckily, in early 2016, Lighthouse received a prestigious Art Tank award from Bonfils-Stanton Foundation and the Denver Foundation's Arts Affinity Group. The monetary support was transformative, to be sure, but it was more important to know that others believed in the transformative nature of creative writing and wanted it to happen throughout the community.

I must also admit: we partly began running adult workshops because we were asked to. A Lighthouse member, William Dewey, who worked for the Department of Local Affairs, connected me with Simone Groene-Nieto at the Denver Public Library. The library was looking to offer patrons a safe space in which to explore their creativity. Simone wanted to specifically address the needs of patrons experiencing homelessness and/or extreme poverty. Thus, the Hard Times Writing Workshop was born.

As of this writing, Hard Times has been going strong for almost two-and-a-half years, and has become one of the library's most popular offerings. Whenever I attend, I'm struck by the camaraderie and care the participants show for one another, and I'm deeply inspired by the quality of the work they create. My heart fills with hope, but I'm not surprised. When workshop participants are dedicated to the process, this is what happens.

Our basic philosophy on these workshops is perhaps best summed up by the author Richard Rhodes, who says that "Writing is a form of making, and making humanizes the world." I would take it a step further: writing is a most effective form of making, because its material is language, our most common method of connection. Writing isn't the only way for us to get to know one another—for us to, as the old saying goes, walk a mile in another person's shoes—but it sure is convenient. And versatile.

Not only do the community engagement workshops celebrated in this anthology nurture the creativity and the voice of participants, the work itself contains great power. As an exclamation of our common humanity; as a voice calling out from the behind walls built out of our fear of the other—the refugee, the senior, the veteran, the person living with illness, the person experiencing homelessness, the person emerging from incarceration. We read and learn: this person has dreams and worries just like me. We're not all that different.

More than ever, it's clear that such work is necessary. Forces of division and intolerance seem to be everywhere; they threaten our common good. Success in battling these forces is hard to measure; it's slow going, one person at a time, one group at a time, one story, one essay, one poem at a time.

We know that creative writing isn't a magic panacea for all the issues we face. It's just one effort in the larger collective. And yet, we have this beautiful, profound, and sometimes raw, collection. I hope you read it voraciously, and I hope you are as moved by it as I am.

To all of those who've supported this effort: thank you. This book would not exist without you. And to all the writers published here, and all the writers who've participated: thank you for your work. You inspire me. And please, keep writing. Keep humanizing the world.

FORT LYON SUPPORTIVE RESIDENTIAL COMMUNITY

KATHY CONDE

Introduction
Empowering People at Fort Lyon

I arrived at the fort late in the evening. I would be spending four weeks as a Lighthouse Writer-in-Residence on the Fort Lyon campus that serves as a supportive residential community for people who have struggled with homelessness and addiction to alcohol and / or drugs. Inside the women's dorm where I would be staying, the institutional halls had been refashioned by the women who lived there—welcome signs and drawings on the doors, a day room with a fridge, a microwave, sofas and chairs that the women cleaned and tended daily, and home-made curtains dressing the large, metal windows. Two of the women escorted me down the hall and opened the door to a room that they, themselves, had made into a homey, freshly-painted room with curtains and a string of tiny lights hung on the wall over the bed that made it look like a welcome party.

That night at 3:00 AM, the fire alarm went off, a piercing blare and strobe lights that had us all rushing out the doors for sensory relief if not fear of fire. We stood around the bottom of the stone staircase in our pajamas and coats for about half an hour. The quad, the size of a couple football fields, was majestic in the half-moon light. Large brick buildings, some with columns, faced the quad on three sides, giving the place the feel of a college campus. When they finally let us back into the building and I saw the metal fire doors still shut on either side of the hall, I felt the history of this place. It had been a prison and before that a VA hospital and a mental institution. That was when I realized how much the current residents had transformed the place.

I spent a lot of my time walking around meeting people and talking to them, mainly listening. Within just a couple days, the residents started telling me their stories when they had a chance to catch me alone at the microwave or the stairwell or out on the quad or after class. They told their stories with candor and clarity, no drama, though sometimes with breath uneven or hands slightly shaking. Some of the stories were of childhood abuse or rape or violence, trauma that could be permanently devastating for any of us. And there were stories of deep loss and insurmountable grief. Stories of abandonment and stories of learning lessons of self-hatred instead of self-love at such a young age there was no defense. Many, very many, of these residents were just like me, but where I had gotten a break they had not. Their stories involved ending up on the street, losing loved ones, losing everything. And they told stories of their difficulties on the street—violence, frostbite that took fingers or toes, run-ins with the law. It became clear to me very quickly that every one of the residents had survived and overcome tremendous obstacles to get to Fort Lyon and to this new sobriety.

In the writing classes I held daily, I was thrilled to see the level of talent and the diversity of writing styles in the participants. And the willingness to engage fully with the writing and with the group—it was like their trials had led them to a place of openness, and their creativity was flourishing. The work they produced was excellent and the atmosphere and vibes in the writing group were more harmonious and receptive and nurturing than any I had ever been in.

During my four weeks there I probably talked with about half of the 200 plus residents. The ones who were willing to talk to me were intelligent and usually kind. They were grateful to be at Fort Lyon, grateful for the opportunity to have shelter and food while they focused on staying clean and sober there. They were getting practice, preparing for life back out in the world once they got their balance. They were grateful to have enough time, up to two years, to become stable in their sobriety, so that when they went back to live and work outside of Fort Lyon, they could have a good chance of being successful, a good chance to stay clean and sober.

One of the case managers explained to me that it costs the state of Colorado more than twice as much per person per year for homeless people to be on the street (emergency room, medical, police, courts, detox) than to be at Fort Lyon. And in 2017, Fort Lyon had a dropout rate of 38 percent, a lot lower than the national average for rehab programs. In my opinion, operating the facility at Fort Lyon is well worth it by every criteria, including a moral one. There are other organizations serving the homeless in other ways, but it was easy for me to see that for the people I met in my four weeks there, Fort Lyon was exactly what they needed.

There is very little that is mandatory for the residents at Fort Lyon. They have to stay clean and sober, and that is strictly monitored. They have to go to three community meetings a week that are informational or inspirational or both. During their first 30 days they are required to stay on campus. And they have to attend a six-week substance abuse education class. After that their time is their own. Most of the residents keep busy with various activities that they, themselves, set up—different support group meetings like LifeRing and Celebrate Recovery and other spontaneous groups with unique focuses. There are also many AA and NA meetings and those groups, set up and attended by residents, pay rent for their meeting space at Fort Lyon, according to their tradition of being fully self-supportive. Residents can also take a shuttle to outside meetings. There is a creativity room at Fort Lyon, where many residents go to paint or build or let their imaginations be free, utilizing the stock of materials provided there. There is also a sewing room, a well-stocked library, a post office, a weight room, a gym with a basketball court, and an extension of Otero Junior College, where residents can take college classes right there at Fort Lyon. Some residents take a bus to La Junta for classes that aren't offered at Fort Lyon. Residents do community service in the area, often in Las Animas or La Junta.

It was a very dynamic and diverse community that I found at Fort Lyon. In addition to all their activities, they also knew how to pause for a conversation. They were the most communicative people I have ever met. I was in heaven since I'm all about communication. It's why I write. At Fort Lyon, all I had to do was show up—in the hall, on the quad, in the classroom—and communication happened constantly. Everyone I encountered there was fiercely working their own individual program for substance addiction recovery, customized for themselves by themselves—from newcomers who were giddy over the opportunity they suddenly had to seasoned residents preparing to leave after two years, sober and hopeful and sometimes sad to leave the place that had become home.

I recently read an article by Will McGrath in *Pacific Standard* from January 2, 2017, where the co-founders of Fort Lyon, James Ginsburg and Phil Harrington, talked about this unique project. Ginsburg, director at Fort Lyon, who has worked in homeless advocacy for the last 25 years, said that "the vision for Fort Lyon was to let the needs of the people who came there drive the structure of the program, rather than create a rehab program and make people comply." The way they set it up was to "allow those in rehab to direct their own recovery." He spoke of "flattening the hierarchy, of empowering people, of inherent human dignity." Harrington, associate director at Fort Lyon, said that "given enough time and space, people find their own way. He described a process he had witnessed time and again at Fort Lyon: People eventually came to realize that there was no one to fool, no one to please, no one to rebel against. Fort Lyon was simply a community of like-minded people trying to help each other." In my time there, I could see that this unique approach was working for many residents.

My last evening there, some of the residents gave me a going-away party with a cake that said Thank You on it. The party was a joyful reunion of many of the people I'd been so lucky to meet and talk with and be inspired by during my stay there. I didn't even know they all knew each other, but of course they did. Looking around the room, I could see they treasured their sobriety and were proud of what they were doing at this supportive place. They were being given respect and responsibility for their own sobriety at Fort Lyon and they were stepping up to the plate. They were, and continue to be, an inspirational force in my life as I aspire to become brave and reach for my own goals and dreams and step up to the plate.

I feel fortunate to have had time with the residents at Fort Lyon and to have been in a fluid and dynamic writing group with some of them. I think we often surprised ourselves and each other with our writing. I'm thrilled that they are willing to share with you some of their writing in this anthology.

ALEXANDRA DONOVAN

Introduction
Writing and Recovery:
The Mystery of Grace

I was lucky enough to spend a month during the summer of 2018 with the residents of the Fort Lyon Supportive Residential Community in Las Animas, Colorado, as their summer Writer-in-Residence. It was one of the most powerful and beautiful experiences of my life.

Most everyone at Fort Lyon is in some form of recovery, and the more time I spent hearing the stories that led into addictions and life on the streets but also the stories of strength and courage and overcoming, I began to get a real glimpse, for the first time in my life, of the world of recovery. It's a world where courage and grace meet daily, and though it's a place I haven't myself lived, it's a place I can recognize from afar, to a small degree, from the not-too-distant shore of my own human struggles, and the writing life itself. I stand in awe, and even perhaps jealousy, of the choices the residents and staff at Fort Lyon make on a daily basis to create a life that is self-aware, humble, proactive, and other-oriented.

There's a quote from Father Greg Boyle, founder of Homeboy Industries in Los Angeles, that I return to often, from his book *Tattoos on the Heart*: "Here is what we seek: a compassion that can stand in awe at what [others] have to carry rather than stand in judgment at how they carry it." The original quote has "the poor" where I have put "others," but the reality of human pain and tragedy is, we could all be poor. We are all the other. And if there's one thing you'll learn over and over again here, it's that it could just as easily be you here. It could just as easily have been you that suffered a brain injury and subsequent intolerable depression, or a home life of abuse that led you to turn to substances to numb out the pain. It could all, so easily, be any of us. I "knew" that, coming in, but every day at the Fort, I knew it more and more in my bones. And every day, I knew too that the grace of our "higher power," whatever that is for each of us, is an offer that is available daily, though some days we may have to look harder or wait more patiently for it. As best I can understand, the theology of recovery is something like this: the underlying illness doesn't go away, but neither does the grace. You can get "off the rails," but you can't go back to square one. Nothing is lost. Every day is a chance for courage and grace, or for failure and even more grace to meet you on the other end. There's a freedom in knowing that perfection is unattainable, and just as much in knowing that progress is possible, and only one step away.

In our community meetings, Fort Lyon's Program Director James Ginsburg would often end his inspirational pep talk by telling the newcomers: "Stick around, and don't leave until the miracle happens." And the miracle will—again and again.

I got to witness small and big miracles almost every day in our creative writing classes. Students wrote poems and prose pieces about addiction, grief, abuse, betrayal, guilt, shame, unfinished business, forgiveness, freedom, hope, despair, beauty, chaos, and glimpses of meaning. They wrote about topics like "the worst day," "what no one tells you until it is too late," the "photograph in my pocket," and the hero's journey. They experimented with erasures, pantoums, rhyme, blank verse, fiction, and sonnets. Every class had its own kind of magic, and even—often especially—when we got "off topic" and changed our trajectory, when we trusted the thing that was ruminating and emerging in that shared space, the miracle happened. Grace appeared in the form of small revelations, creative surprises, moments of awe, openings for grief. The three poems included in this collection are beautiful examples of that grace.

"The Worst Day," by Jason Sweeney, was the result of a conversation that Jason and I had during office hours in the Fort Lyon library. Jason came to talk to me because he is interested in writing a young adult novel about addiction some day, something I truly hope he does. I gave him some prompts that might help him jumpstart some scenes. The prompt he chose to write from was, "Write about the worst day." What resulted, to my surprise, was an intricately crafted poem that took me right into the heart of his most intimate grief, a moment that has shaped him and haunted him. In the poem, the speaker wrestles with simultaneously knowing, and not believing, that his father's death is not his fault. The ambiguity in the third line of the final quatrain, "a self-delivered .38 slug's impact did reverberate," is not in my mind accidental or incidental. The bullet is "self-delivered" by the father, but it sounds at first as if the speaker has delivered the shot. In talking with Jason after he showed me this poem, I learned that he carried tremendous guilt about his father's suicide. He believed his father, who had always wanted him to be less studious and more athletic, had been deeply depressed partly, somehow, as a result of his seven-year-old self. My heart broke when Jason told me this, and we talked about whether he still feels that way. He told me, "It's a really old wound. That's kind of hard to shake." The self awareness in this statement, and in the poem, was humbling. This poem shows me the way that writing allows us to powerfully re-inhabit our own stories, to own them, and also to set them on paper so that we can take a step back and observe our own psyches. This is the ultimate privilege of being a teacher: I am allowed into windows into my students' most beautiful and tragic moments. Poetry both takes us there and also gives us a way of return. It allows us to mark the territory, to tell ourselves we will not forget, and it lets us see where we are standing, sometimes more clearly than ever before.

"Heart Shaped Rock," by Sam Guymon, was written during our class session on "writing from nature." For this lesson, I brought in a selection of objects from the natural world and set them in the middle of our conference table. I always like gathering new objects from the local area before I do this lesson; it gives me a chance to listen a little bit to what might be calling to us from the world around us even before class begins. In class, we read and talked about examples of poems that use the natural world as a launch pad, a "triggering topic," to get into deeper material. We then talked about "turns" in poems, the places where a deeper subject matter may be revealed, when the poem suddenly becomes more than it was. I asked the students to begin writing about any object that called to them, to describe the object and really let it start to speak to them, and then at some point in the poem to introduce a specific "you." The you could be an ex lover, a friend, a parent, a dog, a self-address...only the student had to know who it was. In some ways, I was forcing them to create a poetic turn. What emerged was pure magic, and Sam's poem was one of my favorite examples of a poem with a gut-punching turn at the end of the poem. It's a beautiful example of the way that image carries emotion, and also of the ways in which poems take us places we, as readers and writers alike, never expected to end up. This poem is its own small, powerful, confessional.

Finally, "After All: An Erasure" by Kathleen Navarich was one of those incredible magic moments that continues to stay with you. That day, I asked students to do a free-write of all the negative things that they had been told, or that they had ever believed, about themselves. I made sure they knew they wouldn't have to share this. This exercise in itself was powerful, and the room was filled with a heavy sort of quiet while the pens scratched away. When students were finished with their free-write, I asked them to create an erasure. Erasures are poems formed by taking a source text (in this case, the free-write created moments ago) and allowing a new poem to lift up out of the source by choosing what words, or parts of words, to keep, then "erasing" (either actually erasing, or blacking out) the rest. Kathleen was almost beside herself to share when the time came, and she was brave enough to read both her original and her erasure, and to share both for this collection. The original text was a reiteration of her "searching and fearless moral inventory," the 4th step of AA. As she read her erasure of that inventory, a collective chill went through the room. I can think of no better example of grace than this poem. When we are asked to lean into the mess of our lives, we discover unexpected beauty already waiting there for us. That beauty is our own voice. By some mysterious collaboration of willpower and divine intervention, a new thing emerges from what we thought to be ruin. We care about ourselves, "after all."

LIZ MATHEWS

Grey Owl and I

From a slow heartbeat in the bed
To a drumroll
To the approval of the spirit
And the grey owl of the night

I have moved to the window
Through it, and to the branch
That called me scratching at the glass
It is a black cat kind of dark

And while my eyes adjust to the dreamtime
To the space-time between masses
My ears hear a howling wind
Like the wild ocean in a seashell

I watch myself asleep in bed
And feel no thread between us two
The Owl comes to lift me down
His wings are mine till I can fly

"We're due to meet the Moon tonight
She's fierce and bold and smells our lies
She'll want know your truths and fears."
With blackhole eyes he beckoned me

In this spell I shed my gown
And accompanied ran to the berm
Where no greater sky was ever seen
And no fuller moon, blood red and blue

Grey Owl of the night and I
Stood small and made our voices loud

With all the freezing air could hold
Our vibrations cut the clouds apart

"Grandmother Moon!" we banshee called
"We've come to offer up our souls!
Our knowingness is that we know less.
Our great fear- that we'll never live again."

It seemed at once the stars rotated
The Moon's bright face shone stark and white
A booming laughter rolled through the air
It took all our strength to not be felled

"Oh sweet Owl, and dear sweet girl!
Were we supposed to meet tonight?
I've been laughing at such cosmic jokes
As the one about Taurus and . . ." she stopped.

"In any case, dear mortal souls,
I've heard your truth and heard your fears.
It is indeed a frightening thing to be alive
And not know past death."

"A more frightening thing - I would imagine
Would be to think you know for sure.
So do not fear, and do not know, and
Laugh always about your knowing less."

With that she turned the sky around
Grey Owl and I flew quietly back
"I thought our interview was today," said Owl
And we both laughed myself awake.

Rob Moorhead

A Portrait in Two Parts

I. Note to Self

I know mom just died. The rest of life is not going to be easy. I have no advice for you, you are on your own. There will be horrible times in your life that you must get through. These bad times will pass but you will have to fight. You will know when you are at these points in time, they will be obvious. I will not try to help or explain a way around these hurdles because then you will not become the amazing person that you are destined to become. You will live, learn, fight, struggle. That is life. And remember, never give up, never give in.

P.S. Stay away from Amy Conforti.

II. Untitled

I am from my mom. Not a place, not a time, not a date. She made me who I am, who I was, and who I will be. I am from her and she will always be a part of my life. I am from her and now hearing her voice and seeing her face, satisfied, at peace at times, but always having thoughts of letting her family down, and myself knowing that she did not. I am from my mom, and now, she is from me.

DON LAWRENCE

One

I've been here before, not seen, even less heard, trying to flee, seized with a paralysis of curiosity, intrigued. Funny how some pursue a kiss from death, rather than admit defeat, this time I up the ante—I'm all in, Hearts lead on this hand—Stay woke—be conscious, no need to redefine, the dialogue of this day—so "cliché" my happiness? Well it's all a lie . . . Potential energy is easily made kinetic, her vibrations—movements. Hers is energy that won't be ignored, the intensity . . . reverberations that would pulsate from the ocean's floor . . . such a seduction with words—words that manifest from thoughts, thoughts so swift the naked eye can't detect a frequency—choose your weaponry wisely! A physical frame that is a marvel, to be celebrated—applauded, as if thunder jolted the land after the lightning, I was pricked by the thorn from a rose that broke the skin—Attempting to walk this tight rope, with no feet, we don't speak the same language, but I bear witness—the sun—the time—the moon—the stars, all dance to your tune . . . I want to keep this blessing for myself—I don't know why, outline your name in the sky, the rush—my high . . . my creator would not author such confusion, or is this mental fusion an illusion? I seek an antidote for the kiss from the black widow—I require her serum, but the signs, and the science are heavily guarded by other culprits . . . my starship departs here, I don't want to time travel anymore, I NEED to be here—this mission—is a retransmission 93 million miles away from, came ONE, more than a movement—a migration, a representation of ONE . . . peace and light . . .

KATHLEEN NAVARICH

Can You Imagine

Can you imagine someone sewing both sides of your stomach closed? Can you imagine someone sticking a tube into your intestines through the tender, soft flesh of your belly? Then being told, "This is the only way you will ever be able to receive nourishment again." Your mouth, forever after, watering for the things you can no longer enjoy, as you lay there craving your mom's fried potatoes. Can you imagine being so addicted to a drug you would "literally" die for it? Your heart would stop, and you would awaken with a searing pain punching through your chest that would leave you bruised for days afterward. A drug so insidious you crave to be released from the hospital just to do some more. My name is Kat, and this is what happened to my baby girl, my daughter Jennifer, and one that I can only imagine. I would like to share with you the hideous insanity of how a drug called Spice / K2 ruined her life: stealing her beauty and love for life, rendering her not much more than an invalid with little desire to live.

I was living in Redding, California when I received a Facebook message from Jenny, my daughter. It read "Momma I'm sick, I need you, I'm dying!" Fear gripped my insides: I ran to the bathroom and started throwing up, tears streaming down my face. Sweating, I made my way back to my computer. I sent a message back telling her I would get her a ticket on the first flight I could find. She wrote back, "I can't Momma, my doctors are here, please come to Denver." I replied, "I'm on my way!"

When I arrived in Denver, I was shocked to see my once beautiful daughter. Her hair was grayer than mine and unbeknownst to me, she had a hole in her throat to breathe and speak through called a tracheotomy tube. She wasn't at all excited to see me and acted very distant, her eyes a dull gray. (My mind flashed a picture of bright sparkling sapphire blue eyes, full of laughter and mischief looking up at me "I didn't let the hamster out Mommy, honest.") She said she needed to pick up her medicine and asked if I had any cash. "Of course, sweetheart, let's go get it," I said. Jen took me to a rough looking area and asked me to wait while she went to pick it up. I immediately knew something was wrong; she said it was for some medical marijuana, so she could eat.

When Jenn returned, she sat on the grass and rolled the nastiest smelling joint, promptly smoking it down to nothing. I commented on the smell, and she admitted that it was Spice not exactly pot (marijuana) like she had led me to believe. I had no idea what it was, but they sold it legally over the counter at the time. She then admitted to me she was on probation and that was why she couldn't come to Redding. Jenn said, "Come on Mom, look at me, jail would kill me." Spice apparently doesn't make you come up dirty when they tested you for drugs and was also the reason why she had to have the tracheotomy. I wanted to know why she was on probation. "I'm not a child anymore, it was no big deal!" We got into a huge argument, and she stormed off, running and hollering down the middle of the street "you just don't understand, you'll never understand!!" leaving me standing, helpless, on the corner. In a town I had never been to before.

I called a taxi, found a place I could afford to move into on my meager disability income here in Denver and proceeded to wait for her to contact me again through Facebook. I waited and searched everywhere in this strange, unfamiliar town, contacting the authorities to no avail, before my daughter finally contacted me again.

Four excruciating long years had passed when in May 2016 my Facebook messenger flashed "Mom can I come see you?" I quickly responded, "Of course you can." As it turned out, she lived just 3 or 4 miles from me and had been for a couple of years, so close and yet so far. I was so relieved and excited to hear from her again, my palms were sweating, and my stomach was full of butterflies.

When she knocked on the door, all the joy in me evaporated, and I started to cry. My baby was so gaunt and haggard, her eyes—flashing the anger and defiance from our last meeting, all I had been able to see in my mind's eye, awake or asleep—now dull and lifeless. She let me hold her for a moment then pushed me away. They had removed her tracheotomy, which I took as a good sign. "Can I smoke in here?" She asked. "Of course," I said. While she was rolling she lifted her shirt and showed me a small tube protruding from the left side of her once firm stomach, zigzagging scars ran like a highway across her pale sagging flesh; I was stunned into silence. Jenn proceeded to light up another one of those joints she called Spice, I caught a glimpse of defiance spark through her eyes, and I was determined to do anything, go along with whatever, just to keep my 38-year-old child, my angel, my precious baby girl, from running away again. She started telling me how her heart had stopped and how three times now she died and woke up in the ambulance being shocked with those paddles. Jenny said the pain had been so unbearable that she had stayed bruised for weeks afterward. Her skin was paper thin, and she just wanted to die and get it over with. "Momma, you are the only reason I have left to live."

As my baby finished her joint, she immediately rolled another one and fired it up. I tried so very hard to endure the awful stench, but I was literally about to throw up, I had to tell her to put it out. "But I need it; it's the only thing that helps my pain. I'm NPO (nothing passes orally) now for the rest of my life." Her voice started to elevate, and I could hear the tremor. "I also have a DNR (do not resuscitate) order." "Jenny, I love you with all my heart and soul, but if you must smoke that, you will have to sit on the porch while you smoke." I just could not condone her smoking it in the house, after all this is the drug that had crippled her. She went outside and sat on the steps. Jenn's coughing stopped, so I peeked out the blinds. She had disappeared again.

Little puffs of cold air escaped my mouth as I walked up to my porch and hurried inside. It had been snowing for several days nonstop, and we had gotten at least 5 ½ inches of snow just over the last 13 or 14 hours. The windows were fogged over from the laundry I was drying, and the fresh smell of coffee I had made demanded my immediate attention. My old bones ached as I drew patterns on the cold glass of my kitchen windows while I sipped coffee from my steamy mug, wondering where my daughter might be. So lost in my fearful thoughts I almost jumped out of my skin when the phone started its shrill ringing. As I hurried to pick it up, I kept saying "please let it be Jenn, please let it be Jenn, please Lord; Hello . . . (silence), Hello" . . . A weak, tiny voice said, "Mommy I'm in the hospital, I'm going to die . . . Help me, please Mommy, don't hang up!" Big fat, hot tears flooded my eyes and dripped into the coffee I had forgotten I was holding. I looked down, unseeing as it shattered on the floor, and sank to my knees. "I'm here my baby, Mommy's here, I'm not going to hang up. Where are you, sweetheart? What's wrong?" My voice shook as my mind said: "not again, please Lord, no more." There was a loud roaring in my ears. Shaking my head I forced myself to get a grip. Jenny needs me. My daughter's words came back to me, full of terror, something I had never heard from her before. "They put a pic in my heart, (she was panting) and my body rejected it, (her words running together breathlessly) it's infected, I have a yeast infection in my blood, and I'm going to die, they have me in the Intensive Care Unit for communicable diseases. I need my Mommy; I need you sooo badly, I'm scared. Please come see me!" I fought to find my voice; I could feel my heart pounding as little flutters went through it and I prayed "Please Lord Jesus, help me," the taste of bile and salty tears in my mouth. I swallowed over and over to keep from vomiting. "Calm down my baby, tell me what hospital you are in, I'm on my way."

As I walked into the hospital, a multitude of smells hit me, and my stomach rolled. I was afraid of what I would find this time, how much more could my daughter's mind and body take. Jenny was as pale as a ghost, her eyes sunk deep in her head, big and round and full of fear. She took hold of my hand with more strength than I would have thought possible and didn't let go. We cried as I held her tight and whispered soft cooing words of comfort and stroked her hair until she relaxed in a fitful slumber. All of this was the result of "Spice."

It has taken three long months of intensive care, and I will never have my daughter back. Jennifer has the mentality of a 6 or 7-year-old most of the time now. I am working on taking a C.N.A. classes so I might be able to one day care for her myself at home. Jenn will never be able to bathe herself again or eat or drink, ever. We are taking it one day at a time, and each morning I pray won't be her last. Spice/K2 is a killer; we need more about it in the media and education in our schools. I speak with people all the time that have no clue how deadly this synthetic marijuana is. They take grass, hay, herbs of any kind and spray it with poisons like wasp killer, and any other chemicals they can think of, then sell it cheap on the streets to our children. Please don't let it happen to your child.

Russell March

I am / Don't Be Afraid to Branch Out

I am a tree
deeply rooted
growing
giving unequivocally
I am a tree
dancing
hugging the wind
filling the air with the sweet scent of Pine
I am a tree
solid
beautiful
unique
I am a tree
a protector
a practitioner of the Fibonacci sequence
I am a tree
I am a tree.
I am not a bucket of ashes.

JASON SWEENEY

The Worst Day

The day the desert sun blazed brightly
wet and glistening I climbed out of the pool.
I thought the time was unremarkable, like any other;
hindsight is twenty-twenty, and I see myself a fool.

As I set across the threshold of my house
I saw friends and family gathered in my home.
Incongruous I saw my mother collapsed and weeping;
though so surrounded, she seemed totally alone.

Her sobs filled me with a sense of dread and panic;
being only seven, I couldn't fathom why.
I had felt her anger, the rod, the lash
but never to that day had I seen my mother cry.

To her side I rushed and asked her what was wrong,
and through gasping breaths and tears she said
with a world-shattering voice, like a banshee's song,
my mother told me: "Jason, your dad is dead."

Frozen in a moment that bordered on the infinite—
hate, sorrow, grief—knowing that I was the one to blame,
a self-delivered .38 slug's impact did reverberate
rending my reality apart. My life would never be the same.

KATHLEEN NAVARICH

After All: An Erasure

I was controlling, close-minded.
I thought the world evolved around
me and it did or I would relocate.

I was self-will run riotous.
I went where I chose, when I chose,
with no accountability to anyone
…not even to myself.

The hardest thing to swallow
was the fact I didn't know it—you
see, I had no inkling. I never
allowed the veil of myself—justifying
 righteousness—to be lifted.

I'm not sure what most people had
to say because I was taught I didn't
care about them; after all it was all
about me anyway.

My friends were my followers or
they didn't deserve the time of day.
If you were negative you had no
place in my life…after all.

I was   minded.
          the world   around
me

was

          where I chose
          accountability
                    to my self

                the fact,   you
see, I had
allowed the veil of myself
                    to be lifted.

                                    I

cared
about me

                        after all.

SAM GUYMON

Heart-Shaped Rock

Dark grey,
flat and skinny
on the ground it did lay
sticking out like a shiny penny.

Two curves on top,
sharp point on the bottom,
It made me stop.
"My precious," said Gollum.

It spoke a strange language,
the universal language of love.
For eternity it will never vanquish;
as is below, as is above.

My heart sank as I watched it skip across the lake
like stardust in the night: black and blue.
I had no clue what was at stake
the day I said good-bye to you.

WRITING WITH CANCER WORKSHOP

MICHAEL HENRY

Introduction
Writing With Cancer Workshop

For almost a year now I've been facilitating the UCHealth Writing with Cancer Workshop, and I've cherished each moment I've had with these writers, many of whom are living with cancer and in active treatment. Others are in remission; two have served as caregivers for a loved one. As happens in workshop sometimes, we laugh and we cry—the latter perhaps a little more than in a typical workshop. And we write.

I love these afternoons here at Lighthouse, in the old, blue dining room. I very much look forward to them. And yes, I am sometimes emotionally wrung out when the class is over and everyone leaves, but it's a good kind of weariness—the ease you feel when you're truly alive and present in the world.

When I was 24 years old, my mother died from lung cancer. First diagnosed during my junior year in college, she fought bravely for three years. During that time, I was broken and grief-stricken over something that hadn't happened yet. At times I wanted to run away from her illness, but I knew this experience was the most important thing I might ever go through, and I promised myself that I would not look away. For whatever reason, this was my life, and the experience would unmake me, and then it would remake me into the person I was destined to become.

You can probably guess that I became a writer. It's a long story, and it feels strange to say it, but my mother's death turned into a gift, one mixed with deep grief, which I feel to this day. I lived this experience and had no choice in the matter, and to deal with it, I began to write. Mostly about how precious life was—every single mundane, foolish, boring, and transcendent moment. I learned to pay close attention, for what is the life you're supposed to lead but the one you are leading, and who knows when it might all disappear? So why not write it all down, to help you remember, to help you make sense of it, and perhaps share it with others?

These UC Health workshops sometimes break my heart, but then my time with these incredibly brave, brilliant people also mends it. With every word they write and share, with their honesty, their fears and joys, all of which shows up on the page. What they write is honest and beautiful, and sometimes it's dark. But just as often it's hopeful, full of tenderness and love, as you'll see.

MARCIA JONES

Daddy—A Trilogy

I—First Time I Let You Go
When you left, I chased
you into Third Street.
The meddlesome neighbor
pulled back her sheer curtains.
Tomorrow she will raise eyebrows
of proper fresh-permed ladies
gossiping in the beauty shop
downtown.

My tears streamed hot,
scorching my face.
My ears clanged like a train
bearing down on a crossroad.

I grew up in that moment.

It was the first time
I let you go.

II—Where Only We Have Been
I have your hands

hands that held me
on the night I dreamed a tiger

hands that sheltered me
in the crash of rain

hands that tossed me
laughing into the air
and always caught me coming down

aged hands
that explored my face
to work out who I was

our hands are a geography
of cracked earth
ancient river beds
purple hills ravaged
with sun and drought

a geography where only you and I have been

III— At the Twisted Frontier
You always turned the other way
when we walked past the door
of the memory care wing.

Don't ever put me in there, you said.

Now we face that door — your new home,
your last home.

Only last year you reflected,
in your small voice trembling
like a white moth sailing
on an early summer's night,

that if you could slip
once and for all
into fading memory's
cruel night, maybe then,
only then,
you could forget, escape
dementia's murky torment.

Now we open the door.
We face your ragged reality together,

your hand gripping mine just as I
trusted yours a whole lifetime ago.

Daddy,
you have lingered way too long
at the twisted frontier of knowing
and not knowing.

Jonathan F. Ormes

Prognosis: Two or three years, but who knows

Your cancer has spread.
I'm compelled to ask.
Prognosis?
You might live two or three, but who
knows.

I heard of cancer as a child.
A family friend dying in the hospital.
I listened, frightened as they spoke of
pain.
She wants to die, but there's no way.

I fear not dying.
I've lived well.
It's pain that threatens, I volunteer.
Doctor kindly
"We have ways of managing it".
My wife is crying.

At this stage we used to do chemo.
I had decided to refuse it.
Now we have some new meds to try.
What will they buy?
Perhaps a few months.

Want to join a study? Choices three:
Nothing; take new drugs; take new drugs
and join study.
Study means more complexity.
Pill rules, logs and an iPad with stupid questions.
Monthly cat scans and the dreaded MRI, banging at me.

Scientist in me rules. Double-blind. It's
hard explaining.
Maybe I am taking a placebo.

Side effects?
Your body will change shape they say
Shrinking, spreading, volume unchanged.
Testosterone forced to zero. The cancer
lives on it.
Hot flashes, enlarged breasts, but voice unchanged.
No more sex, but that's long gone anyway.

If you ask me now, "I'm feeling fine"
Or, maybe I'll say, "OK."
Do they really want to know?

Years ago I'd heard my surgeon say
I hope to save your nerves.
Mostly you will relearn
to control your bladder.
Don't sneeze or laugh unexpectedly.
I still don't trust the catchment pad.

Appetite is great. Let's out to dine.
She likes that. Food is the new sex.
I'm not so good at losing weight.

The grim reaper is following me
Two or three left—enjoy!
Friends and family more intense.
Shared the news, but now it goes unmentioned.

My pain and aches are kept at bay.
Miracle drugs, expensive, covered I know
not how.
You don't believe in evolution?
Mutation will eventually lead to malignant growth.

Beloved spouse is really stressed.
We plan a move to a retirement
community.
Activities to distract when I am gone.
They keep asking if I'm depressed.
 But her burden isn't of concern.

Every day is time for a nap
Sitting in a lounge chair by my bed
Covered by the quilt made of old T-shirts
I try to read, but it never lasts.
I can't keep my eyes open.

I spend my life in the bathroom.
Radiation from an earlier phase
Has left my bladder with a cyst.
It bleeds and scares me.
Dr. seems unconcerned, so it must not be fatal.

Strength is something I've not got.
We're heading for retirement home.
Nothing but old people. Friends and
relatives are helping with the boxes.

My last scan showed blockage of an artery.
It went unmentioned by the Doc.
But I have no appetite for exercise.
I have to remember to try and walk.

My thoughts turn to the grim reaper.
I implore
Don't wave your dull blade of fear
Use the sharp blade of certainty
Your scythe once wielded, make it true.

Maureen Ackerman

Love, Brimming

Once, I'd have preached to anyone who would listen that the purpose of life was to die in the state of grace, to suffer through like the martyrs and offer it up. Now I see it this way: You're not born to die in grace, you're born to live in it. You can lift those stones of sadness, you can lift them to the light until they shine, you can spin them until they sing, until your life beats like so many iambs and spills like a poem to the page, where it keeps forever.

The small white house where I grew up was built in the mid-1940s on the vast potato fields that once were Westbury, a shingled box just like the few hundred others that eventually sprang up along Whittier and Lowell and the other little streets named for poets. The O'Haras and Corcorans and Kellys were returning to Brooklyn from the war, and out on Long Island, Mr. Levitt was building them a dream that danced against city streets, luring the men to trade the courage of battle and the limits of their Brooklyn parishes for the expansive promise of St. Brigid, patron saint of poets and sweet saint of compassion, who would look with kindness on the more subtle courage of their longing hearts. So they came east, and we Sweeneys came with them, settling into Poets Corner and shaping our single selves out of our common cloth, threads woven of prayer and guilt, story and silence, fathers who strayed hard, mothers who suffered harder, and a generation of daughters and sons who would wander, in time, from the saints.

But first I wanted to live like the saints, to be like the children of Fatima who saw visions of the mother of God. I wanted my name to be Lucy or Cecelia, a worthy name, not Maureen, named for the weather on the night I was born. It had rained forever, my mother told me, a Noah kind of rain, and October 10 was no different from the rest. More rain. Maureen. I had come into the world in chaos, my older sister, Gael, liked to put it, I had come not quite complete enough to keep up with the world beyond my mother's body, my four pounds confining me to an incubator until I'd gained enough weight to go home. From there, I suppose, came the story I would learn to create, the myth I would construct for how and who I would be to make up for how I began.

I would be good.

At 75, I believe that my family noticed my efforts, but I have little memory of praise until my mother wrote a poem in my eighth grade autograph book, one I immediately memorized and recite to myself, still, when I need to:

> Day after day, I've watched you grow
> In beauty and wisdom's light.
> May God keep your heart always aglow
> With love for Him, burning bright.

I finally realize that, for long stretches, they were carrying their approval with their other secrets like a suitcase of stones. I lived inside that silence, and I did not ask why.

I listened instead. The kitchen was just in front of the room I shared with Gael, and if I lay bone still in bed and curled up close to the wall, I could hear my mother and the various ladies who drank coffee with her elevate opinions to articles of faith as sacred as the scapular or

Friday fish. By the time I was fourteen and suffering through my first earthly crush, I had learned more than I needed to know about marriage and its minor miseries. Marry a Protestant, Mrs. O'Hara warned, and you get a weekly Bible lesson. Marry an

Italian, you get the family for Sunday gravy. Marry an Irishman, you get his mother, for as long as she lives and then some, while he works out his guilt. My mother got Nanny when she married her Frankie, and though Nanny outlived her by two years and my mother never got to know if Mrs. O'Hara had been right, this much is true: My father died from Parkinson's, his body a bag of tremors but his heart still beating its history, guilt hanging around him like a fog that he couldn't push through.

Perhaps if my parents had moved somewhere else in Westbury, to one of the brick houses on Breezy Hill, where men in gray pants and undershirts and women in black dresses and hairnets pinned money on the Virgin's velvet robe every August; or if they had found a split-level in Salisbury, where families named Cohen and Klein sent their kids to summer camp; or if the little capes in Poets Corner hadn't been bordered on the north by the Long Island Railroad, in walking distance from our house; perhaps then Nanny couldn't have arrived each weekend to fill the house with her stubborn self, winning my affections while filling my mother with simmering rage.

I don't remember waking up on Saturdays. I remember only the whistle announcing the 10:35 from Flatbush. Finally they would appear, Nanny always in the lead. Nanny never walked, she waddled, side to side as though she'd been raised on the sea. Laden with shopping bag in one hand and tied green Ebingers boxes in the other, she waddled purposefully, her lipsticked mouth set and determined. Spring and summer must have happened in the 40s and 50s, but I remember Nanny as a winter lady, mink collar of the black wool coat high to her chin, mink hat and its pearl hatpin partially protecting her graying curls. In step behind Nanny trudged Kuke, half the width of the woman he followed, equally laden with weekend supplies. Kuke carried the grips, though, never the food. The food was Nanny's.

From the boxes came the sweets: French crullers, all sticky vanilla on the outside, wet, wet yellow in; cinnamon buns, raisiny and sweet; crullers, twisted and powdered and long. And from its own box came the yellow cake, seven layers high, iced in light chocolate and almond slivers. From the shopping bag came the rolls, hard ones with seeds, and then the Flatbush butcher's baloney and pot roast and beef cubes for stew.

Tucked under the stairs was the round, front-loading Bendix, and as the machine whirled, Nanny whirled, from cabinets to counter tops, sponging everything she could reach. Then room to room she'd streak, dust rag and polish in hand, bullying dirt as she bullied my grandfather to "get in here and work." Shaking away the two minutes of sleep he'd stolen, Kuke would jump to comply, but even the dirt learned to defy him. Scrub though he would, yellowing tiles refused to whiten, metal cabinets refused to unrust. By evening, though, when we'd glory in her goulash, even Nanny would sit for a while, begging for praise. "What would you do without Nanny?" was all that she needed to know.

For years the question hung in that kitchen and in all the rooms of the little white cape, answered only by Nanny herself and the ritual cleaning and feeding. When it was at last addressed by my mother, the red-headed daughter-in-law to whom Nanny's Frankie had pledged devotion, it wrote itself in a stinging resentment that shaped, in its sadness, the rest of our lives.

But in those early days, when the train streaked so close you could catch the conductor's salute, and Saturday nights stretched long with bingo or board games, what Nanny probably never knew was that she and Kuke were giving me a merit system I could understand. Virtue was easy, and it came with a reward. Sneak Kuke an extra beer, I'd get a quarter shinier than his old bald head. Bury myself in the fat folds of Nanny's arms until I smelled like Evening in Paris with her, I'd get a shopping trip to Woolworth's the next week. Not rules, exactly, but a sense of what was expected and a prize that proved I complied.

When I was ten, I earned the grand prize of all, the Infant of Prague statue with the crown of jewels and the brocade robe that ruffled under the chin. For two hot weeks of July, while Gael went to Point Lookout with Aunt Alice to look for boys at the beach or stay up all night reading, I went to Ocean Avenue in Brooklyn, to Nanny's hot apartment house, where I spent most days riding in the elevator with my twin cousins from Philadelphia, or playing hide and seek in the musty stench of the basement washroom. Gael was fourteen and wouldn't go to Nanny's anymore, just like she'd no longer hug anybody who wore toilet water from Woolworth's, but I was still collecting the holy cards the nuns gave instead of stars for perfect papers, and I was falling some little bit in love with Jesus of the soft brown eyes and wavy hair. Nanny had a hundred Jesus cards, at least, and a whole dresser top of statues she told us about before bed each night. The twins took St. Anthony back to Philadelphia to help them find their jacks and marbles when their brother, Joey, lost them to his friends. I came home from Brooklyn with the Infant of Prague, whose face was whiter than a communion wafer and was sweeter against my lips when I kissed it good night than anything Gael could taste on a boy, even the one whose sweater she wore home from the beach, along with a sunburn and loose peels of skin.

St. Brigid School had real rules and a system as strong on demerits as Nanny's was easy on rewards. I must have sensed early that the way to survive lay in total acquiescence to Sister's commands. I raised my hand, I memorized my Middle Atlantic States, I filled my mite box, and I sold my chance books to the same neighbors whose kids were selling theirs at my house. I memorized my nutshells, I diagrammed my sentences, I practiced my Palmer script until it was as perfect as Sister's, and I wore my scapular humbly. But oh, how it hurt to be humble. The scapular promised immediate and eternal salvation if I died while it circled my neck, an easy insurance policy, I could sense even then, if ever I should stray from the saints. At fourteen, Gael was becoming as wild as the March wind the night she was born, and she had already strayed out of our room and into the upstairs attic space, where I had seen the stash of movie magazines under the clothes on her closet shelf when I brought up the clean wash. She was in public school by then and without a uniform, and there were no dirty silk strings peeking out from the sweaters she buttoned down her back, so I alternately prayed for her soul and showed off my own smug sanctity by wearing the scapular outside my white blouse, but she only yelled louder at us when Annie McLoon came to play, and slammed the door.

Eternal salvation notwithstanding, my temporal sufferings in search of sanctity were an agony no scrawny little girl should have had to endure. Despite my absolute compliance in all matters related to Sister and school; despite the dubious distinction of achieving star pupil status; despite even the coveted glory of best explaining *What the Rosary Means to Me* and crowning Mary in the sixth grade May procession, there was something I couldn't do, not even for the nuns.

Each year in the beginning of school, Dr. Behm came in to weigh and measure us. I came home one day just after I'd turned seven to find my mother cutting cheese cubes at the kitchen table, crying. Sister had called, she told me. Sister had told her I weighed only thirty-five pounds and that second graders had to be bigger than that. Why didn't she feed me more, Sister had demanded, why didn't she make me eat? I had run home through the cemetery between school and our street with Dickie Higgins like I did most days and had been ready to meet up for beanbags after milk, but there was my mother coaxing cheese cubes into me and promising me through muffled sobs a malted with egg just like Mrs. O'Hara liked because Mrs. O'Hara was skinny, too, and malteds were a way to get fat. The cheese was dry and it crumbled in my mouth and then I cried, too, I cried with all thirty-five pounds I carried that please, it wasn't fair, I'd try to get fatter, I promised I'd get fatter, even though it seemed that I'd choke before gaining one more ounce on this strange, unmanageable earth. But I chewed the cheese and I swallowed and I prayed to become big.

My prayers didn't work. May came, and First Communion, and I was still small and led the line into church with Dickie Higgins. My mother was crying again because I was sick with tonsillitis and couldn't take the pink medicine Dr. Behm had given me until after I'd had the host. I was crying again because I had to cover the eyelet sleeves of my communion dress with a shawl and nobody would see how they capped at the shoulders. Sister didn't care that the day was March gray instead of May blue and told my mother that I couldn't wear the shawl or even the crocheted white sweater from Nanny, I'd have to suffer the cold like everybody else and offer it to Jesus. By the time we sang to the Lord that we weren't worthy to receive Him, I didn't know if He'd ever speak the words of comfort we were seeking and heal my spirit, or my body, for that matter, no matter how many malteds my mother made me drink. But I sang all the words, I sang from my heart and swollen throat, and as Sister clicked us through the Mass so we'd know when to sit and stand and kneel, I prayed that the wafer would slide on my tongue past my teeth without touching so Sister could stop being mad and my mother could stop crying and I could get on with being good.

Gael, meanwhile, had her own way with the nuns, who saw past her scarcely veiled insolence to the curious brain that was already rumored to hold more information than their own, and they treated her with a respect usually reserved for the pastor or mean Father Flynn. Gael had been reading *even in the crib*, as Aunt Alice put it, and she could do the times tables in her head, so she was often dispatched during fifth and sixth grade arithmetic drills to the seventh and eighth grade classrooms, where she would take Sister's place behind the big brown desk and show off her skills, pronouncing even the hard words in the history books without stumbles.

Maybe that was how the nuns kept her questions away, by keeping her out of the way, but by the time she was in seventh grade, the beautiful child with the angel-white skin and hair the color of sinking sun had stopped performing, even for Sister. She sat through school with her classmates, but she was already someplace else.

I was still struggling to be good, but in seventh grade I suffered my own crisis and fell from grace, hard. To celebrate the new school finally built across town, and to reward us for selling enough chance books to include a chapel on the first floor, the Sisters had organized a religion bee to determine which single student from the seventh and eight grade classes best understood the religion that would save us from both far and near occasions of sin. I had happily memorized every word in my Baltimore catechism and could recite on command the answer to any question Sister asked. I was an obvious candidate, but I had obviously sinned, laughing along with my classmates about a bald-headed mouse and singing with happy conviction about old Mr. McDermott's garden that June was busting out all over, though I did wonder every time what could be so funny about anything as beautiful as the red and pink roses that I pressed my nose into when nobody was watching. Not until years later did I know it was thirteen-going-on- eighteen June Davenport that the boys had meant.

Word had reached Sister that dirty jokes were spreading through her classroom with greater fervor than indulgences, and after inviting Father Flynn to remind us of Purgatory and the long torment of the sinful soul before it could be happy with Jesus forever, she had demanded, and received, confession of the crime, at least from me. I didn't know what that mouse meant, but it had made even serious William Gannon double over, so I suspected I was guilty of something.

On the day of my disgrace, I faced my public humiliation with a shame proportional to my spelling bee trophies pride. "Your name is MUD!" Sister announced in front of all seventy- six of us waiting for our afternoon geography test. We had just come in from the parking lot where we were allowed to play dodge ball or tag after our baloney sandwiches, when Sister burst through the door and swept across the front of the room, her long black dress collecting chalk dust and her rosary beads clattering like angry teeth through the stunned silence around her. "You cannot represent this class!" she screamed when she reached my seat by the window, and then she leaned toward me, her face red and twisted against the stiff white wimple of her habit. "Shame on you. Now we have to find someone else. What do you say?"

This was Sister, and I couldn't speak, I couldn't look, I could only bore a hole with my eyes into the desk so I might disappear. But Sister wouldn't let me. Pulling my chin toward her and demanding that I look smack at the spittle collecting on her lips, she screamed on about the bee, the bee, only four days left until the bee.

"Please, Sister, I'm sorry, Sister," I managed, but my words were weak in the hushed air, the classroom by now a held breath while Sister turned back toward her own desk and the catechism book with the questions. Then she lined us up and began the drill.

Why did God make You?

Name the four marks of the Church. Name the gifts of the Holy Ghost.

Again and again, Sister hurled us the questions. I knew the answers, I knew all of the answers, and though I tried not to say them, they would not be stilled. I had learned that book by heart, and I was last standing again.

Perhaps others confessed, too, and that is why, despite my grave mistakes, I was finally allowed to compete in the bee. Or perhaps Sister wanted the glory my first place finish might garner, erasing from Father Flynn's memory her class's momentary lapse. According to the original reward system, an eighth grader would, of course, win the contest, collecting as prize a year's tuition to the Catholic high school of his choice. But I, a seventh grader, had learned my catechism too well. I received a daily missal with silky strings that I own to this day, but I did not receive the scholarship. I also did not attend the school with the winding staircase named for the Sacred Heart. Instead, I ultimately selected the public high school in which "all kinds" enrolled, a secret I dared not disclose to Sister until my General Excellence medal had been pinned securely in place.

Bedtimes were, the sky had lit up like halos, a whole heaven full of saints to watch over me while I slept. But the sky was changing, the stars scattering like punctuation through a story called *How Things Move*, shifting into question marks against the dark page of night. I had wanted to trust the nuns forever, to be holy and perfect and pure, but something in me was moving, too. It was tugging like a hand on a curtain cord to let in the light, daring me to wonder about the unfathomable shift of the heart, how it ever learns to live its brimming love.

SUNNY BRIDGE

You

You are missing from me.
That's how the French say it –
Tu me manques –
As if I have to tell you of your absence,
As if the fact of where you are not is enough.
But somehow, translated,
My broken heart is lost along the way
When we leave this language of love.

You are *missing* from me.
But there you are
Just beyond the veil.
I hear your voice in the silence,
In the space between the ache and the cry.
The scent of you on the last pillowcase you used
Nearly drowns me with longing some nights.
I gasp and drag in breath after ragged breath,
Burrowing in,
But it's not enough.
Never enough.
That part of you *has* died.
And yet . . . .

And yet . . . .
You are not the ashes in the cognac box
You are not the poster on the easel in the corner of the
vestibule.
You are not even the scent on the treasured pillowcase or on
the brush in the bathroom drawer.

The essence of you,
Just beyond the veil,
That part of you cannot die,
Can never die.

But can you hear me when I confess that
You gave me wings I never really tried
Or rather reminded me that I had had wings all along.
Is it because you are here
And yet
Not here
I want to spread them now?
I want to soar,
But not *to* you, I think,
Not now. Not yet.

That time has not yet come.
But maybe *because* of you,
Thanks to you.

You are missing from *me*,
That is true,
But I wonder,
Am *I* missing from *you*?

HARD TIMES WRITING WORKSHOP—
ARVADA PUBLIC LIBRARY

Joy Roulier Sawyer

Introduction
Hard Times Writing Workshop—
Arvada Public Library

The story of the Hard Times Writing Workshop—Arvada Public Library begins with its sister pioneer, the Denver Public Library Central branch—a workshop I'm also privileged to help facilitate. Several years ago, I visited the group and first encountered its brilliant writers, as well as its remarkable facilitator, Jane Thatcher. I've been part of the DCPL writing community ever since.

Some might think I use the word "brilliant" loosely. But I remember how mind-blowing it was the first time I heard these writers read aloud their fresh, unpretentious work and give feedback to others.

Several volunteer editors from Lighthouse have told me about the misconceptions they held before first attending one of these workshops. They expected to hear mere self-expression; instead, they witnessed a level of writing that challenged their own.

And then there's Jane. I've led many community outreach groups before, but never before observed a more gifted, savvy, and prepared facilitator. The warm, positive environment, the structured format, the challenging literature and prompts—all created by Jane. Actually, Hard Times is Jane. When I first began facilitating the Arvada Hard Times workshop, I merely followed her thriving model.

The Arvada workshop hosts several of the city's slowly-growing population of those experiencing homelessness. Before its inception, a nearby church, The Rising, opened its doors as a day shelter across the street from the Arvada Public Library—the first gentle nudge that a Hard Times workshop was needed. We held our first weekly Wednesday session in January 2018.

The workshop meets in a gorgeous second-floor room at the library, with floor-to-ceiling windows that provide a spectacular view of the mountains. The warm aesthetics of the room provide the perfect, soothing environment for the writers.

From the time the Arvada Hard Times workshop began, we've hosted a strong core of 12-15 regular attendees. Lately, we've attracted several younger writers. The workshop is a solid mix of those facing homelessness or housing challenges, mental health issues, Naval and Army veterans—as well as other community members currently experiencing "hard times."

The group is so diverse that one day, an older white veteran shared a moving piece about his last days on his tour in Vietnam—while a young Canadian Asian refugee read a story about her family revisiting that same country, many years after they'd fled the war in terror.

Like the writers at the DCPL Hard Times, these participants are also brilliant, well-read, and diverse. Also, like the DCPL workshop, the group consists of differing beliefs on politics, religion, and culture. They work hard to maintain an atmosphere of safety and mutual respect.

In our workshop, we cover a wide variety of readings and prompts—anything from parsing the first paragraph of George Saunders' short story "The Tenth of December," to writing in response to a wacky, random prompt like "The moon made me do it."

Several Arvada writers have progressed to take Lighthouse workshops, some of them advanced. This past February, Stories on Stage presented "Voices from the Edge," a celebration of writing from the Lighthouse outreach writing workshops, with pieces selected by the actors themselves for performance. The Arvada Hard Times writers had the most pieces chosen.

But perhaps just as important as the writing that takes place is the deep spirit of support and community that exists among the Arvada group. The writers share with each other mental health resources, job leads, and computer help outside the workshop.

Also, in addition to the generous snacks provided by the library, some writers bring their own homemade goodies to share: fresh chocolate chip cookies, or even meal items like individual pizzas, egg rolls, or goulash. Other participants bring extra canned goods, or fresh apples and peaches from their backyards.

Many say the encouraging workshop environment has improved the quality of their creative work. "I'm writing about more specific, sensory, concrete details," says participant Trish Veal. "I don't have to worry about how my grammar or spelling errors will be received instead of my actual story.

"The Hard Times workshop is my weekly 'therapy,'" she adds. "It has helped me work out some of my issues with others, my grief from many losses, my current pain over experiencing homelessness. It's given me some of my power back."

Working with the Hard Times writers is one of the true highlights of my life. In fact, I dedicated my latest poetry book, *Lifeguards*, to them. "TO THE DENVER CENTRAL LIBRARY AND ARVADA LIBRARY HARD TIMES WRITERS—FULL OF LIGHT," it reads.

Its facing page contains the book's epigraph by Thomas Merton: "There is no way of telling people that they are all walking around shining like the sun."

DANIEL ANGEL MARTINEZ

A Hard Times Poem

Are you expecting soothing words in life?
Have you not learned to read between the rhymes?
A poet's pen can cut a slice of strife,
Reminding us each day of bitter times.
Do you rely on moon and starry nights?
Tell me then, what's with all the dark in space?
It seems this life, in truth, has dimmer lights.
My words of gloom are gems that I embrace.
Extolling darkness I can find recourse.
So sweet the sounds without the noise of day.
Perhaps my muse will help to find the source.
On fragile wings my soul will blaze the way.
Ejecting flaws and blahs now brings about
My words to read to speak without a doubt.

DANIEL ANGEL MARTINEZ

Come See America

Come see America through my eyes
        and you will realize
I build the beautiful cities that bring in the clamorous crowds
        and off the highway
        my barrio peeks through
        industrial clouds.

Come see America through my eyes
        and you will realize
I feed the hungry masses, it's no miracle or trick;
        bound to hellish fields—
        a brief coolness in every
        cucumber I pick.

Come see America through my eyes
        and you will realize
I serve in the military—put my ass on the line—
        used to dirty work,
        no stranger to the trenches,
        these hands of mine.

Come see America through my eyes
        and you will realize
        sacrifice,
            struggle,
                survival.

Come see America through my eyes
        and don't be surprised
        if you see
            your future.

MARIANNE REID

Peeping

Late that night, it was quiet in the living room when I began to hear faint peeping. I sat still, to listen and determine where the peeping was coming from. I pulled the base amp away from the wall and peered into the back of it. I saw a nest of fluff. It contained six baby mice, pink, no hair, eyes closed, and peeping.

My mind leapt to that morning when I had found a dead mouse in the trap, a dead mother mouse with her teats full of milk. I felt badly that her babies were now motherless, so I decided to take up their care, much to the consternation of the relatives visiting from the Midwest.

I concocted a recipe of mouse formula to feed them, straight from my imagination. Wild mice are rather vicious. I took up each one by the scruff of their pink wrinkly necks and fed them with an eyedropper. Each one would struggle and try to bite until they got the taste of food. Their bodies would relax and hang from my fingers, with just their little tongues lapping.

I realized that wild mice cannot be tamed in one generation. They are as mean as Tasmanian devils and slow learners. They grew their silky mouse fur and opened their shiny button eyes, only to glare at me in mistrust. The mice ate solid food and still hated me.

I came home from work one day and found my mice gone from their cage. My unthinking husband had decided they were big enough to release in the bottom pasture. I would have preferred to let them go myself, and watch them disappear into the grasses.

ROBERT PETRICH

The Evolution of Speed:
A Fictional Character in Neil Simon's
The Odd Couple

They call me Speed. I grew up in lower Manhattan, the seventh son of eleven kids. My father started running numbers when he was sixteen before becoming a bookie at the Italian- American Social Club on Mulberry Street. He had a reputation for accuracy and faithfulness to his boss, Joseph Bonanno. Dad did nicely until the feds got Joe Valachi to break the code of silence surrounding the New York Mafia.

I went to Fordham to earn my accounting degree. That's where I met Oscar Madison, a journalism student a year older than me. Oscar's kind of a lovable slob and we hit it off. He got a summer job writing advertising for the Brooklyn Dodgers and was paid mostly with beer and baseball tickets. Oscar and I went to a lot of games and he taught me about player performance and tendencies. I took it from there, applying statistical analysis to the matchups. I was soon setting the odds for baseball betting parlors around New York City.

Even though I'm good with numbers, my passion is being a player, not a bookmaker. My favorite game is poker. I love working out the odds and the angles and trying to beat the house. The best feeling in the world is playing the rush when the dealer works fast and the cards come out in your favor.

At first, I found poker relaxing, a stress reliever from my accounting job in the financial district. I looked for friendly games where I could sit in, like Oscar's on Friday nights. But the guys started thinking I took it too seriously. I admit, I got irritated when the game didn't go the way I wanted. If I'm losing, I want to speed up the game and win back my losses as fast as I can. If I'm winning, I want to speed up the game while my luck lasts.

When Ernst & Young found out I was more earnest about poker than corporate balance sheets, they offered me a severance package and I took it. I used the money to buy my way into legal tournaments in Atlantic City and high stakes underground games around the east coast.

I promised my wife I would try professional poker for a year and quit if I didn't break even. I lied. After a year, I borrowed money and sold my wife's wedding ring to stake myself. She divorced me when we lost our apartment in the Village.

Greenies were something I learned about when I studied baseball performance back in college. I discovered those little green pills could help me stay focused during overnight tournaments. That's when I started wearing dark glasses. I never liked anybody studying my face when I was playing. Now I'm afraid they might see the amphetamine in my eyes. I hope they don't start drug testing poker players like they do the ponies at Aqueduct.

I'm in too far and can't quit now, not when the next tournament could make me a winner. My motto remains, "If I got a chip and a chair, I got a chance." So, Lady Luck, put on your Hollywood gown and heels for me. Be my higher power in the room. If my red cards are beaten by a cooler, turn my black cards into money. And please don't leave with someone else tonight.

Saoirse Charis-Graves

Cottonwood

The old cottonwood dominates at the edge of the field.

Beyond my flagstone patio embedded with a secret spiral path,
Smooth round river rocks in one corner,
A terra cotta chiminea in the other.

Beyond the steep bank of rocks,
Clumps of stumps foreshadowing a summer's battle
to tame the persistent and unwelcome willows that block
    my view.

Beyond the dribble of a narrow creek
Swelling with runoff every spring
Soothing sounds of water over rock.

Beyond the back forty
Untended and wild
A plain of weeds and more awkward clumps.

Beyond the fire pit, a real pit with a circle of stones,
A circle of random tree stumps and boards for sitting,
Ashes from decades of nighttime storytelling.

Beyond, a neighbor's cat is buried at the roots of the old
cottonwood.
He suffered the death of one too far roaming
For our local den of coyotes.

The cottonwood stands at the corner of the wooden post and
    rail fence
Separating "us" from "them" - "Out there"
Beyond the fence, beyond the tree.

The old cottonwood fills my eyes each morning
As darkness lifts
And my hope rises yet again.

SAOIRSE CHARIS-GRAVES

Liminality

Pulled to the image
She stands at the edge of the flagstone patio
Drinking in the moon
Full and glowing
Casting a cool light on the field behind her house
Drawing a stark silhouette of the large cottonwood
At the far edge of the field
Blotches of trees up on the bluff
The horizon a sharp line between ground and sky

Above the uppermost reach of the cottonwood
Between the moon
And the tree's fingered stretch toward heaven
A single star takes its place
Claiming the sky
On behalf of all the other stars
At this moment yet unseen

Cheeky star -
Daring to show up
the moon's bright glow
With it's own radiance
Albeit lesser
Still compelling in the dark sky
So perfectly set between
The flat black silhouette of the tree
And the pulsing luminosity of the moon

Still, she wonders.
What is this juxtaposition
Of moon and tree and star?
What compels her to this moment?

Mary Oliver would know the meaning
Of the black bodies of the trees
Against the glowing sky
The vivid presence of a single star
Hung in between
The dark and the light
The ground and the source

She is left to wonder
To stand waiting Breathing
Rocking back and forth

She will let the words settle in the night
And rise with the dawn.

Saoirse Charis-Graves

Waking Dream

They wait for me,
A circle of blank canvasses,
Squares of white against a background of fire red—
My waking dream.

Beyond my patio
In the angled early morning light

Softer than the full sun of midday
The leaves of the cottonwood at the far edge of the field
Flicker In the breeze
Like the dappling of light on water.

The native grass
Waist-high
Seedheads forming a feathered finial
Atop slender stalks
Swaying to a silent rhythm.

Above the grass
A flotilla of fluff
Floats on the breeze
Lifts and drifts
In search of the perfect landing spot
A growing place for the new cottonwood
That wants to spring up
Along the creek just beyond the patio.

A small bird
A sparrow perhaps
Skims the top of the grasses
Pauses on the rock atop my chiminea

Scouting a likely cache
Of insect bodies
More breakfast for his tiny stomach.
A larger bird
The tell-tale red epaulet on black wing Foraging nearby
pumping wings
In heavy contrast to the lightness of the sparrow.

Faithful Jasper lies on the patio
Turns his head to follow the birds in flight
Lifts his nose to sniff the air
Turns back to look at me.

I've left the back door open
So he has options.

The sparrow bravely perches
On the back of the chair
Just beyond the dog
And chirps at me.
Yes, looks at me and chirps.
Cheeky bird.

Yes, I know.
A while back it was a cheeky star,
And now a cheeky bird.
I like a little cheeky in my life.

I wonder.
What have blank canvasses
In a field of red
To do with cottonwood leaves,
Swaying grass,
And a cheeky bird.

JANE LEWIS

The Effect of Gamma Rays on Man and the Moon Marigolds

The community had gathered together. Farmers came in from the fields to wash up and take their families to town. The city kids and their folks moseyed on over to the hall, where neighbors greeted each other with jokes and storytelling before finding their seats. The hall would soon be filled with presentations in dramatic interpretation, poetry, duet acting, speeches and improvisation performed by the local high school forensic students.

Forensics saved me from the boredom of small town life. Every Friday afternoon after school we would board a bus with our forensics coach and travel around Kansas to competitions. As a freshman, I performed a dramatic interpretation from the book *Black Boy* at the state event and won a gold medal. From then on, I was hooked and became a fierce competitor.

With the end of my senior year approaching, coach decided to have us perform for the community and in costume. My duet partner and I met back stage to get ready. I donned a dirty half-slip and an old bathrobe and slippers. Disheveled hair paired well with the mascara streaked down one side of my face. A half empty whiskey bottle dangled from my left hand completing the costume. My partner plastered her face with heavy makeup and wore a short, cheap looking dress. The curtain rose on the last act of the night—our intense drama selection. When it was over, there was a long moment of silence and then wild applause.

After a costume change, I made my way outside and was greeted by coach who gave me a bear hug. "That was your best performance!" As I walked towards other friends expressing congratulations, I heard my partner yell, "Jane!" I turned to see her approach me with tears streaming down her red, blotchy face. Through choking sobs she murmured, "Mummy and Daddy are ashamed of me. I've disgraced them in front of our family and friends. They forbid me to hang out or speak with you again. You're a bad influence." Once their message was communicated, she abruptly turned and walked away.

I stood there motionless not quite comprehending what was going on. Then the realization that her parents - good farming people - couldn't distinguish between acting and reality hit me like a slap in the face. It stung and at the same time was a compliment in a sad, twisted way.

On the ride home, all I could think about was what a way to lose a friend.

Sheree L. Downs

A Chance Encounter with a Sign Waver

"Oh yeah, there's one and I'm in the right lane for once."

I bet you aren't as happy as me to see a sign waver by the side of the road. You see, I carry what I call "hand-up" bags in my car. In a plastic bag there is: a bottle of water, a packet of noodles, a pouch of tuna, a pouch of peanut butter, some hard candies, a sandwich bag with a knife, fork, spoon, a granola bar, wet wipes and napkins. I also include a note that says, "Things WILL get better-you must believe that. GOD loves you and so do I! Prayers for you." Most importantly, I include a small Bible. It has just the New Testament and Psalms in it but is just the right size to put in the bag, I even carry some pouches of cat and dog food, just in case.

Lately, it seems, I am always in the wrong lane to get to someone or I just haven't seen anyone. So, when I see the guy sitting by the side of the road, I pull into the parking lot and grab a bag.

He looks up at me as I get closer, stands up and smiles at me.

"Hi, I have this for you. I call it a hand-up bag," I tell him.

He looks at me, puzzled. "Why do you think I need one?" he asks.

Oh dear, have I made a mistake? Was he just waiting for a bus?

"I saw the sign, I'm so sorry," I stammer as I back away.

"Wait, don't go. What sign are you talking about?"

"The sign on the ground, right where you were sitting."

He looks to where I'm pointing and we both look closer. It isn't a sign, just a piece of cardboard with HEP on it.

"Wow, I'm really sorry. I thought you were a sign waver and it said help," I turn around and start to walk away.

"Please wait, I'd like to know more about your bags, maybe I could use one, talk to me."

I turn around. "What do you mean, maybe you could use one, are you homeless or not?"

"Let's go over there and talk. I'm Bryan, by the way."

"Okay, I'm Sheree but I want some answers."

We sit down at a nearby bench and I hand Bryan the bag. He opens it and examines each item. As he reads the note, I see tears in his eyes. Bryan looks up at me.

"You don't know how much I needed to hear these words today. Yes, I am homeless; I just didn't want to bug anyone today for a hand out. I was feeling like no one cares about me."

"Oh, but GOD cares about all of us, never give up on him."

"I know that, really. I guess I just needed to be reminded. I'm so glad you stopped."

Bryan asks if I will pray with him, "Yes, of course I will."

As Bryan prays thanking GOD for me, I say a prayer thanking GOD for Bryan and for hope.

I give Bryan my address and he tells me to expect postcards from him.

A week later, the first one arrives. Bryan is still on the road, with an extra item in his backpack: a full size Bible. He says he is reading it cover to cover but some days he will just open it up, point to a verse and it is a verse that speaks to him that day.

I still give up my hand-up bags. I try not to just hand them out the window. I pull over and really talk to the person. I've heard a lot of real stories and everyone lets me pray for them. I don't just see a sign waver anymore. I see real people just like you and I.

Trish Veal

Waves

Chittering of squirrels
Acrobatic Activity
Tree sways without wind

VAL U ABLE

Accentuating the "u" in Gratitude
. . . and the Gratitude in You

Having learned of the health-enhancing effect gratitude has on our physiology, I resolved to retrain my brain for automatic reset to said subject, no matter the crisis.

Case in point: Upon a recent realization I had spilled my drink all over the floor, rushing out the door, my initial reaction was to think, "oh no!" immediately followed by " . . . and I'm grateful for . . .gravity!"

My brain proceeded to bolster my mindset by expounding: "If it weren't for gravity, I'd be frantically chasing this liquid all over the house, perhaps ascending a ladder to reach it all!"

Upon retiring for the night, I reflected on the ease with which my newly acquired cerebral ruts redirected a potentially frustrating occurrence into a positive, refreshing vantage point, healthier both for me and those whom I inspire.

I'm grateful that I'm grateful for gravity.

ANNE MCWHITE

The Last Man Standing

The day started out with such merriment. Shopping for and planning a party featuring steaks, salmon, Greek salad, fruit salad and strawberry shortcake. My nephew, the self-appointed chef, firing up the coals. This kind of feast makes you wonder what the other half is doing. Needless to say, the anticipation was worth the wait. Everyone sitting around watching the night sky, the telescope primed for capturing Saturn, Venus and the moon. We even caught a view of the International Space Station orbiting by. People all engaged, talking and exchanging ideas. People all feasting and sharing a drink—tongues loosened—all giving voice to their opinions. Some voices louder than others depending on their deafness or amount of alcohol consumed. Eventually one by one they disperse. Those with no problems. Those who can recognize enough is enough. Those with caring companions. Those who have a career their lives filled with purpose and friends. They all went home. That left standing alone and isolated the troubled one. The one fighting demons so dark with senses numbed, speech incoherent and angry, and the stumbling drunken gait. Can't let go of those demons; he is the last man standing.

BENJAMIN ERIC NELSON

Exploding Kane

Compliment rejected
Faith concerned about life essence
Direct hit
The heart constricts and bleeds
Tears of acid rain explode
Glass jar of water crystalizes
The storm
Weathered but surviving
A cross of vapor able to sterilize
Able to circumcise
Cut off
Disabled and working
Hell has a nicer bar, but where is the bourbon???
Down a shot
Then water on the rocks
It's okay just put the pipe down
Someday...
We'll all be shocked...
Listen to the sound!!!

HARD TIMES WRITING WORKSHOP—
DENVER CENTRAL LIBRARY

JANE THATCHER

Introduction
Hard Times Writing Workshop— Denver Central Library

When Lighthouse asked me to teach a creative writing class for community members experiencing homelessness and poverty, I jumped at the opportunity. This was a perfect meeting ground for my skills as a social worker and as a creative writing instructor. It would be called the Hard Times Writing Workshop, a nod to Charles Dickens, and to the "worst of times" that many Denverites were experiencing. I loved the idea for this workshop, but when I sat down to think through our first meeting, I panicked. What would I teach? Who would come? What would we do for two straight hours every single week?? There wasn't a curriculum or a template for a community based class like this. I was all nerves walking into our first workshop. Which, honestly, seems fitting. The Hard Times workshop has become a place where we all come to strengthen our voice, and I am no exception.

I vowed to listen to the community. To ask a lot of questions about what they needed, what was working, and what should be fixed. How could we help them? What brilliant insights could I generously bestow upon the participants? Luckily, the writers have been patient with me, and not surprisingly, have taught me far more about writing than I have taught them. I wanted to share a few of the most profound lessons that I have learned from the Hard Times writers, though there have been too many to recount here.

Being seen, and named as a community member, is one of our greatest needs.

We are adept as a society at ignoring large swaths of the population. Pretending like certain social problems don't exist, like some of us are more real than others. The Hard Times writers remind me that being seen and valued within a community is a necessity, even for those of us who are more typically housed. As such, we start all of our workshops by saying our names out loud. Each person introduces themselves and is invited to tell the group what they are working on, or their astrological sign, or their favorite memory of autumn.

Writers need a consistent, safe place to share their work. Every week in Hard Times we gather to share stories, poems, essays, songs, and histories. We gather to hear ourselves in each other's work. I have watched myself and others flourish with the opportunity to be heard so often, and with kind regard. The world is noisy. We are fortified when someone takes the time to listen to our voice over the noise.

There are no gatekeepers. Volunteers and professionals that visit Hard Times are always surprised at the quality of the writing and craft discussions that take place. Our participants know that despite the establishment's best efforts, it can never manage or control the arts. We will write regardless of prestige, or education, or money.

An artistic family is invaluable. Our writing group has seen each other in and out of jobs, and in and out of housing. We have been together through grief and triumph. We have celebrated published work, encouraged blossoming new writers, and cheered for housing opportunities. Perhaps most importantly, we have learned to name each other accurately. You are a writer. You are a poet. You are an artist and your work is worthwhile. So many people show up for the first time in our workshop and sheepishly tell the group that they are "not really a writer." An artistic family reflects back to you the value of your story, and the legitimacy of your voice.

Thank you to the Hard Times Writing Workshop—Denver Central Library for these lessons, and for helping me find my way as an instructor and writer. Thank you for sharing the colors of the parades in New Orleans, the sound of your mother's voice, and the smell of war the first time you landed in Vietnam. Thank you for the chocolate thieves, the bamboo grove poets, and the tobacco smoke winding around your memory. We are in debt to you, and the courage with which you share yourselves and your stories with the world.

LEW FORESTER

Thin Air

All day we've been dazed and blinded
by columbine and paintbrush, by light
tumbling down hillsides. We climb
to an abandoned silver mine, played out

almost a century ago, collapsed and rusting
in mud and flowers. How much more life
can be mined from our bodies, how soon
before we're finally emptied of words?

Once above tree line, I want to linger
in bare altitude, even as marmots bark
unwelcome from rocks, dark clouds move
across remaining snow. In your unrest

you'd flee these skies fast as streams
trickling downward under crusts of ice.
I'd give you the peace of your own wild heart.
I don't know how else to heal you.

DR. JIM MOSES

Untitled

The High Holidays were upon us. The family always gathered at Grandma's house for the Jewish New Year Rosh Hashanah meal. We always looked forward to her cooking. All of the holiday dishes were culinary works of art.

Born in Denver, on November 19, 1885, Sarah was small in stature, four feet ten with dark frizzy hair, very large busted and considered corpulent. I never remember a smile, or a laugh. She was a tyrant. Charlie her father was the Shaman, who tended medically to the poor Jewish people who lived under the viaduct because they couldn't afford homes. His wife Clara was the midwife and gave help to any woman that needed her. Great Grandfather Charlie was a rag picker by profession. He drove his horse drawn wagon, back and forth over the viaduct picking up and delivering the rags Clara had washed. They had eleven children and lived high on a hill on Grove Street. Usually they got paid with chickens, eggs, and produce grown in the area.

The preparation of the meal began a week or so before the holiday. There were always several gourmet entrees and all the fixings to go with them.

About two weeks before the dinner, Grandma was taken to the fishmonger on the West Side of Denver. Someone always had to take her, as she never drove. It was a long trip to go over to the

West side of the city using the Colfax Viaduct to get to his shop. The roads were unpaved and there were still horse and buggies used for transportation, along with automobiles on that side of town. This was where Grandma would always be taken to get her live fish to be used to make her famous Gefilte Fish from scratch. She would walk slowly from tank to tank, and pick out the fish needed. These fish were the cheapest fish he carried. They were usually bottom feeders. Carp, and crappies were her favorites but she shopped for the least expensive to make her final product.

The fish were placed in a crate and covered with very wet towels. When she returned home they were placed in the bathtub until it was time to make her specialty. When I was very young, I loved to go over to Grandma's house and see the fish swimming around in the bathtub. I could touch them and try to catch and squeeze them. But they were always too slippery for me to grab them.

She killed the fish with a heavy wooden mallet, knocking them in the head until they were dead. Then they were all boiled in her large pot together. The fish were boned and skinned. The stench from this part of the preparation was horrible, even with all the kitchen windows open, and the breeze flowing through. The fish were chopped and ground up in her large hand cranked grinder. Then the mixture was spiced, and chopped onions were added and the mixture was rolled it into many large balls, about the size of a cup. Covered tightly, they went into the refrigerator. They were cooked slowly the next day after the mixture had compressed, in spicy water that became the jellied broth that she spooned onto each piece when serving.

She had a large garden at the far end of the backyard, where she grew many of her vegetables and spices. She grasped and tugged two large horseradish roots from the ground and brought them into the kitchen to be washed off. She also picked three large carrots and a bunch of parsley. These were to be an accompaniment to the fish dish. She chopped the horse radishes and then ground it all up fine in the grinder. A large beet had been cooked in advance;

peeled and quartered it went into the grinder and then was mixed with the root. This gave the mixture a beautiful purple reddish color. Sarah took out one of her Bell canning jars and scooped the horseradish into the jar and closed it as tightly as she could hoping that the hot powerful tasting condiment would not lose any of its strength. It brought tears to many of the guests' eyes as they ate the fish, and still they relished every morsel. Second helpings were often called for. The fresh parsley and carrot slices cooked in the broth decorated each plate.

When the day finally arrived to go to Grandma's house, I remember going into the house, and the smells were deliciously overpowering. After whiskey and wine was served, everyone went into the dining room to be seated. It was a beautiful room with a windowed walnut breakfront holding her china, crystal, silver, and linens. The Gefilte fish was brought out on small plates. There were ohs and ahs, and lots of watering mouths when the fish plates were placed. After finishing the wonderful delicacy, a steaming bowl of chicken soup was the next course. It often contained kreplach. Small flat dumplings filled with ground meat. Then the main meal was passed around. Roasted beef, chicken Fricassee, and savory vegetables in many forms. Also served was sweet noodle kugel with raisins and potato kugel, both cooked until crunchy and crispy on the top. The food was passed around the table in what seemed to be an endless circle. Everyone filled their plates high with the delicious dishes that Grandma had prepared.

After a few hours or so of eating and talking and laughing, out came the homemade desserts with many varieties of cookies and pastries. My favorites were rugelach, stuffed with raisins, nuts and fruit preserves. Mandelbreidt, twice baked hard cookies with raisins and chopped almonds, sprinkled with cinnamon and sugar. Lemon sponge cake and honey cake appeared with coffee and tea, but no cream, Grandma kept strict Kosher laws. Some people were so overstuffed with food they had to ask for help getting up from the table.

The family always enjoyed coming together for fun, food, and conversation anytime there was an occasion that we were invited to Grandma's house.

LEW FORESTER

The Waiting Room

Four green walls with poppy prints,
dated, dog-eared magazines,
algae clouded glass of an aquarium
where even the fish seem to wait
for their names to be called.
Where were we before this room,
before cancer, before this earth?
Did we descend from crystal cities
to a world where get well cards
stack up like dirty dishes?
Did we travel in weightless bliss
along avenues of light, instead
of these dim, metastasized lanes

that lead to more waiting?
Where were we and what
will we do with our earthly
hours, good health if it returns?
Hope insists that these walls vanish,
poppies emerge from their frames.
The aquarium will collapse, fish
swimming like rogue cells
back to their murky source.
Our waiting moments will rise
to the sound of a voice that calls
us by our first name and says,
your life will see you now.

Dr. Jim Moses

Untitled

And I thought about you

Often during the day I have a thought about you. I don't know where you are, what you are doing, if you have a job. I don't know if you are using or if you are safe.

When you were five or six years old, we walked around the block. Grandma and I holding one of your hands. We laughed and talked and everyone got some exercise. There was an old house converted to a place where boys in trouble lived until they could come back into society. The name of the organization that ran this new housing facility for boys was called "Stout Street". The boys were all outside in front smoking cigarettes. You always slowed down and looked at them. Your neck craned upward, your flaming red hair was lit up by the sunshine, and you said, "Those are the Smoker Boys". As fate would have it we often visited you when you were in trouble at one rehab time or another at a wonderful place called, "Stout Street" fifteen or so years later. Now I think you have worn out your welcome.

And I thought about you

Yesterday, I went to my writing group at the Denver Public Library. It is sponsored every Tuesday afternoon by Lighthouse's Hard Times Workshop. I have been going every Tuesday that we are in Denver. I am not sure it has improved my writing skills, but

I am learning a lot about humanity.

I seem to be the oldest of the regulars of twenty or thirty people. Others drift in and out. They welcome anyone from any strata of life. Only older teens and up are allowed. The group is generally made up of poor people down on their luck. Some are not necessarily poor but in a difficult space. Homelessness, drugs, ex-convicts, mentally ill, and perhaps others in forms of recovery, or not. I believe all walks of life are represented at some time. One would have to be present to grab the full meaning of these people. We write, we share, we have suggestions to further our writing abilities. It is an unbelievable experience that always leaves me thinking or perhaps even writing, as in this case.

When I walk past the people congregated outside the front door or toward Civic Center Park, it is a sad sight. I think, "Will this be you someday? Will you ever kick the habit? Life is short my grandson, and very precious." Then I recall the recent commercial on TV. "My son had a torn rotator cuff from a football accident", she began, "they gave him Oxycontin for pain. He died many months later of an overdose of Heroin."

And I thought about you

Yesterday, as I approached the front door of the library, there was a young woman perhaps eighteen or twenty, blonde pony tail nicely dressed in a bright red print dress, howling loudly and crying in the arms of a young man. His arms were tightly holding her very closely to him. Stroking her and her hair softly. But she continued to sob her heart out to him. The tears were rolling copiously from her eyes. He was fit, tall, dark, and handsome with a nicely groomed full beard. He gazed out into space as his caresses continued to cradle her upper body. I wondered what possibly could be the true cause of this scene.

Up to the fourth floor where the Hard Times group, was beginning to gather. Hi Ben, Mark, Mike, Janice, nodding to others that I recognize but in my dotage don't remember names as I should. After the doors open, I take a place at the table, asserting to myself not to be last again this week to share whatever I had written that day. I get nervous while waiting to read.

Yesterday, trying to digest my huge pastrami on rye sandwich that I ate the day before with my three high school old "cronies", I was also juggling the scene in front of the library and the TV commercial about the dead young man who overdosed.

And I thought about you

Midway into my writing, the glass doors to the room opened. It was so slight that I didn't stop my prompted writing assignment. Finally I looked. A young woman had begun unloading all of her worldly possessions into the corner. A luggage carrier containing some plastic bags, a bed roll, and several other cloth bags stuffed to the hilt. She walked quietly over to the table where the coffee, water bottles, and snacks, were displayed. She didn't seem to realize that the coffee pot made a hell of a lot of noise when activated. Most eyes looked up from their work, and then quickly went back to writing. I watched her from the corner of my eye.

She was short and very malnourished looking. Her skin was a pale sallow color. Her hair was brown and chopped very short. She was wearing a small gray beanie. Her shirt was old, dirty, and hung very loosely from her body. She wore no bra. Her pants were wrinkled and soiled. She had on old worn fatigue boots laced above the ankle. I could see her hands and forearms were dark from dirt. Her eyes didn't seem to blink, and she held her hands in front of her, as if she was scrubbing them. She took a cup and poured several tiny cups of cream into her coffee, followed by a lot of sugar and three snacks, and sat at the table. No one looked up or stopped their writing.

"That's it folks. Time to get ready to share. Who is sharing today?" Hands raised. "Oh, I see we have a new person who just came in. Please tell us your name." "Mary," the girl looked down at her hands in front of her on the table. "Welcome! Mary," Jane replied.

And I thought about you

I laughingly said, "I have been last or next to last for the last two weeks! I just wanted to share that. "OK," Jane said, "We'll split the table and start with Joyce and then you will be right after Ben." "Deal," I replied with a broad smile.

Joyce read another remarkable piece. "Any comments? Jane asked. "Remember we only give positive feed back, unless otherwise requested by the reader."

Mary was standing at the refreshments and began to speak before anyone was able to raise their hand. No one moved or said a word. Mary's eyes rolled and bugged out severely. Her comments were quite good, but she couldn't seem to bring them to an end. Finally, Jane said, "Thank you for your comments," and went to the next speaker. Every time someone finished sharing, Mary repeatedly began her comments out of turn. Jane began to cut her off and nicely moved on. At one point Mary asked to read something she had written previously. "We'll see," Jane remarked. "Let's see how the time goes." Mary must have been on some powerful drugs. Her mental condition was very sad.

And I thought about you

LEW FORESTER

Screened-in Porch

We enter with sun still flush on our faces
to the distant sound of a mower, the sugary

scent of lilac. Our bodies must be likewise
fragrant, as insects collide with the screen.

The evening light glows amber—we rub
it on us quickly, take seats around

the large glass table. How close yet how
vast the spaces between us— toasting life,

while last year's leaves and countless other
deaths surround us, swept into corners.

Cardinals sing above the great, green lie of cut
lawns, their bright notes sounding long before

and after us. Someone decides hope and desire
are what moves us forward—their words spiral

away from the dissolving moment like laughter
and the clink of glasses. How well our appetites

chase away shadows. How always green this love
we carry, as we gray before each other's eyes.

FRAN FORD

The One with the Problem

Leaning over the bridge at Speer and 6th
gets me sunlight riding slow current
rain-sated, sleepy, cool, and limpid
as a spill of hueless jelly on a long slide

among islets of prairie grass,
and it gives me a look at large gray rats
glad on the glide from frowsy fronds,
algae-frocked rocks and soggy shreds

of floating fast-food sacks.
Too, it offers plastic bottles a-bobble
and soda cans sunk in nooks of sunshine,
a recycler's ready hoard of hap.

The creek returns my frown, my looking down.
Guess I'm the one with the problem.

SHERYL LUNA

Woodland Mosaic

Pine tree and Baby's breath,
trees canopy the garden.
He said to write as if I were planting seeds,
soil black beneath my nails.
The path filled with people carrying backpacks
and water bottles. The irony is plastic
amidst shadow, light and blooming roses.
Purple lotus in a pond so murky with algae.
I imagine the beginning of all life, but we are here
now listening to the voices of young men
talking about old people. A granite rock
solid and seemingly carved beside me.
Wishing I were as stolid, wishing I too
leaned over beauty as a leaf. Bees along white
lilies and rose petals opening hover in droves.
I am wishing I could subdue my mind peacefully.
If I could see blue sky and clouds each day
I would live heaven's white breath. I want to believe
in heaven, but find it beneath my feet, here
in tall grass. Trees loom large in this place,
bare branched in places, lush elsewhere.
Life and death intermingled in every glance.
My own cells frolicking, white they fade
back into the empty air soon enough.
Every cliché comes to me knocking on humanity's
small hope to live. We are as cicadas and crickets,
the sound of our own voices in the background
seemingly whole with the universe's single song.

SHERYL LUNA

The Path

May your gratitude be bold
and naked on the streets of your life.
May you find the holiness of your shins,
the spectacular lines of your wrinkles,
the edge of the universe in your smile.
May your heartbeat sound the celestial
mystery of creation. May you bring
joyous gifts before sour men and dilapidated
beings. May winter make you happy.
Walk with your feet kissing the dirtiest path.
Walk fearlessly mindful. Return to the stillness
within, the home with no doors, the home
with open windows, the home with no gate.

Resolve

Will it be the word with which everything is solved?
Probably not.
Is it worth the effort? Probably so.
Is it problematic? Definitely.
Will it pay dividends? Perhaps.
Win or lose you still must choose.
Discipline equals accomplishment or so we are told.
Sing praises or denials, what usually remains is pride.
Resolve. You know you will feel better if you try your best.
No pain, No gain. No effort, complete shame.

Linda L. Magnuson

Capone and the Seamstress

I was working at the Chicago Tribune in the 70s. The job was collecting money on past due personal ads. I met Corky there. A proud Black woman that didn't take crap off anyone. Working with the public can be stressful. You never know when one will go off the rails. Corky and I formed a friendship and started taking lunches outside the office. It gave us a break from the daily grind. One day we began to talk about our families. Corky started to tell me about her grandmother. It was one of those stories that is passed down through generations and becomes lore.

It was during the Great Depression. Things weren't hard, they where bleak. Her grandmother was able to get a job at one of Capone's brothels as a seamstress. She cared for the working girls' clothes. Washing, pressing, and mending when a client got too frisky. Anything else that needed this kind of attention. This allowed the family to sustain their basic needs. A roof over their head, food on the table, and clothes on their backs. One day, there was an unexpected knocking on the apartment door. When she opened it, there stood two of Capone's soldiers. Only one of them spoke. He explained that they came with a job offer from Mr. Capone. He had heard good things about her. She was a hard and diligent worker, honest, reliable. Most importantly, she never gossiped about what she saw or heard. Mr. Capone would like her to manage one of his brothels.

Corky got that Cheshire cat's smile on her face. Now we're getting to the meat of it, I thought. Her grandmother told the two soldiers, "Please tell Mr. Capone I appreciate his offer. I'm very grateful he thinks highly of me. However, I'm a good Christian woman. I'm afraid there are several duties that I would not be able to do in good conscience. The major one is the selling other human beings." They nodded and said they would reply with her answer. Corky said her grandfather would animatedly enter the conversation at this point. "She just said no to Capone. No one says no to Capone. I thought we were all dead."

A few days later, another knock on the door. The same two soldiers stood before her. Corky said her grandmother told she froze for a moment. Knowing this could fall on either side of the fence. The one who had spoken before began to speak again. Another message from Mr. Capone. He understood why she could not take the position due to religious beliefs. He wanted to assure her and hers that there was nothing to worry about from him. Corky told me the whole family was greatly relieved. Apparently they hadn't been sleeping well.

After all the high drama, her Grandmother began to receive gifts from Big Al. Every holiday she would receive a gift basket filled with enough food to feed her extended family. Corky said she couldn't prove it, but she thinks Grandma always prayed for Mr. Capone and his immortal soul.

BENJAMIN ERIC NELSON

My World Transforming

In the sky of clouds
Pressing onward
Cough drops
Airplane
My world transforming
Losing sight of the future
Another stone turned

Incubate the deceased
Infinite tears
A loss too great to bear
Why can't there be the love???
For all worthy friends
Sin like a thorn in my side
God I tried
Lost sight
Got back up and lied
No regret
Just difficult decisions
To be put into a box
To be remembered
A lot
To find time
Time for compassion
Close my eyes
Wish for a surprise
Like the earth giving back
A bird
An egg
Love of what I create

Michael Sindler

Blanket Justice

It's a crime to own a blanket
when you're sleeping on the street.

You can lie on the bare sidewalk
           slick with ice
          and cushioned only
with the grey slush
                      of foot-beaten snow
      your only clothes
          becoming soaked,
                      then frigid
      as the temperature
          both external and internal
          drops.

You can try to catch your
                      visible
      halting breath which
                      cloud-like
blankets
      the air in front of your face.

You can try to flex muscles and joints
      that are becoming less
                and less responsive
          due to hypothermia
knitting your fingers together as you
          blow on them
                to keep them from
                      becoming totally numb.
          But to own a blanket . . .

that is just too much.

It is an affront to those who have
                 blankets and beds
          and homes and property
                    and positions of respect
within the community.

It is an affront to those whose
       credit cards and bank accounts
              show that they are worthy
                 of owning comfortable quilts
                 and warm
                       soft clothes
       to protect them.

To protect them as they travel
       from home to car
                 to work to car
          to home to car
to shop and dine
       to car to home
                 and repeat again.

To protect them as they walk by
       sneering
                 at those "lazy bums"
who . . .
       torn apart in ways they cannot understand . . .
       the ragged shreds of the woven cloth of lives
          (perhaps also once comfortable
                 as a warm blanket
          or from the beginning little more
                 than scraps of thin sheeting)
       are nothing more

than a windblown nuisance,
an untidy eyesore polluting the streets
their tax dollars pay to keep clean.

That blanket must be ripped away
and taken as "evidence"
of the crimes of being

homeless

helpless

and hopeless.

It will be taken away to a "holding center"
where it will be lost
among the hundreds of others
piling in a room
far warmer
far drier
far more sheltered
than the place occupied by the
shivering
stranded soul
from whom it has been taken.

That blanket will not be covered
by a natural blanket of frost
with its crystalline patterns of decoration

will not gather fresh falling
blankets of snow
or hard pelting
sheets of hail.

It will not change its color
or its hue
turning blue like the lips
and red like the eyes

nose

and cheeks

and pale white like the sallow skin

of the hands that once gripped

at its frayed edges

the weathered face it once

shielded from the wind

the aching

tired body

it helped to keep alive.

What a terrible crime it is to own a blanket.

Almost as terrible

as the crime of taking one away.

To this latter crime . . .

"shame on you" I say!

THE GATHERING PLACE
WRITER'S GROUP

COURTNEY E. MORGAN

Introduction
The Gathering Place Writer's Group

The Gathering Place Writer's Group is a group of women and transgender individuals using creative writing to cope with and transform their experiences with homelessness and poverty—and to empower themselves through self-expression. The Gathering Place is a daytime drop-in center for women, children, and transgender individuals who are experiencing poverty or homelessness.

The group has met every Thursday for the past two years to learn, write and build community. One member won the Denver Woman's Press Club's Unknown Writers Contest, two were selected have their pieces performed by Stories on Stage, and the group as a whole was selected to share a reading and performance at RedLine Contemporary Arts Center's 48 Hours Summit.

The Gather Place Writers speak and write from the margins, from a place of being erased, undervalued, and unheard. And so, word by word, they carve out a place for themselves, a home, where there is none. As one author wrote: "When I write, I am at home / A place that can be full of love or dread, / But it is home // And from this home / I write to you / So that you may see and hear / So that you may understand."

SANDI MARTINEZ

Swayin' Shirley

Turning onto Colfax Avenue, Shirley swears to herself that one of these days, she really is going to do it. She's gonna stomp the pedal to the floor like the old days when she drove the I-25 route, and just—*vroom*. That first burst of speed will be delicious. She won't ever lift her foot again. She imagines planting her toe, and then her foot and her leg becoming like a trunk of a tree, with deep roots. When she hits that first thing—and she *will* hit something, oh yes, she won't be on no highway at all, but on this damn city street—it will be as if flowers blossom out from her head.

The funny thing was, she had played a tree in that very first recital, *Nor'easter in the Garden*. She had listened pouty faced as skinny Mrs. Carlisle, the ballet instructor, had whispered to the man who was doing the costumes, "Shirley here is short and stocky, rather have Nancy or Sylvia do it, but they're our Roses, naturally. Guess she'll do." Shirley could still hear Mrs. Carlisle chanting *Sway, Sway, Sway*! at her in an exasperated, breathy voice, could still remember the surprisingly strong teacher's unsuccessful attempts to get Shirley's short and thick arms to be as long and graceful as the other girls. Shirley thinks of her awkward body moving from side to side, a tree blowin' in the wind. That final leap, when the tree, bested by the storm, fell dramatically to the ground. She practiced for weeks, Shirley recalls, and she nailed it too.

Her Daddy had told her Mama, "Them fancy shoes are too expensive for Shirley to be a god-damn shrub in the background." Still, she had kept up dance for awhile. She never was in a role anything close to Garden Swan, that was true, but she had loved it. Her body still has that muscle memory, not for steps, but for driving down a road. She knows just the right way to move during curves. Her legs are built for speeding up and slowing down, and she prides herself on perfect timing.

It was that homeless man that set her off this morning. Crumpled bus ticket revealing itself, vivid against a dirty palm, and then dropped carelessly on the floor. A snobbish woman with an armload of "fragile" shopping bags, "Could you please wait?" A few stops back, she had let Mr. "I had no idea this pass expired last year" past her post, but mumbled under her breath, the year is printed right there, clear as day.

Thinking again of her notion of mowing down creation, Shirley suddenly has an absurd vision of her bus, sporting downy white angel wings, soaring through a blue sky, complete with fluffy white clouds. She's still behind the wheel, but here, there are no passengers and she can whoop and roar with glee. The Angel of the Bus.

The seat belt around her waist seems to cut. Soon she will need to start her daily regimens to keep her mind from going plumb crazy. Her go-to is a game she calls "Second Pullers." Ol' Shirley' got eyes like a hawk, they can go back and forth from the road ahead to the interior of the bus just like that.

A person—known as the first puller—yanks the cord for a stop. Then a second someone, ninety-nine percent of the time sportin' headphones, unaware that a stop was requested, will pull the cord again. They don't hear the ding, or the cool automated voice telling them the intersection of the stop. That moment of panic, even if it lasts only a split second, is another scrumptious thing. Shirley makes sure to eye the road instead of the second pullers looks of relief when the bus makes its stop.

Then there's I-Spy. She must spy a woman wearing red. Or three funny hats. A man that could be a pirate. She has no rhyme or reason to who she must spy—it's simply whatever floats into her head. It's often weird or difficult, but Shirley loves a challenge. When she finds her mark after a long day of searching, her sense of accomplishment is much greater than what amounts to the simple task of getting people from point A to B.

She drifts back to the clouds. She's not behind the wheel anymore, but gracefully pirouetting, extending her legs to the ceiling, even through the emergency exit! The bus glides in and out of the clouds. A dancer. Today she must spy . . . a dancer.

White flurries float softly down and pile up. The day wears on, coats and scarves wrap bodies, and Shirley thinks it might be difficult to spot the one.

Shirley's eyes finally flit to her prize during her last run. A stand out, as if struck by a spotlight. The thin-as-a-beanpole young woman waits patiently at the end of a line of people waiting to board. A small duffle bag slung across her chest, which Shirley will bet on her life contains the sacred satin footwear. A thick sweater over the young woman's frame, Shirley spots a bright purple leotard poking through. Long legs, which must be pointed in her trainers, draw circles in the snow. Bouncing outwards in quick *pliés* a few times, to keep warm perhaps. She does a sort of prance up to the door. Her hair is pulled up messily into a top knot, secured with a frilly pink flower barrette. Humming to herself as she shows Shirley her ticket. The girl declines another passenger's offer of a seat. Now it's *relevés* as she holds the upper rail strap and the bus takes off. Shirley loses track of her, doesn't see where she gets off, but she's mostly satisfied, though she wonders if the young woman is a first or second puller.

A child and her mother begin to run across the street, though their crossing light is red and Shirley's is green. Shirley is a good distance away, plenty of time to stop if she needs to. For a brief moment she wants to follow through with her fantasy, speed up, damn everybody and everything. You cross when you're supposed to cross. Become the dark angel. Yet so vivid, like the dancer's flower barrette, she sees her flying bus, now surrounded by smoggy, acrid clouds. A horrible plummeting sensation, her stomach in her throat. She's ended up in a fiery chasm, dark air. She'd better change the tempo of her step.

Back at the depot, the day is done. Tomorrow there will be other passengers, maybe another storm. Might as well keep going, retirement is only a few years away. Shirley, after shutting off the engine, the lights, and pulling the key, pauses at the top step, looking left and right. No one is around but old Joe the mechanic, she won't care if he sees her. Her heels spring up and down. She thinks of roots pulling apart in a shower of dirt. She leaps gracefully through the bus door, her legs forming a perfect triangle, her toes pointed, and lands on the pavement below.

LETICIA DARLINA TANGUMA

The Wolf Under the Street Light

I loved looking into his eyes. I saw the universe in their deep brown richness reflecting nebulas and fleeting comets. I saw infinity. As he looked back at me, it felt like he saw something, too. His eyes filled with tears. The moments passed with gentle impatience and with a mixture of shyness and sacrifice. He looked into the future knowing with innocent absolution that every wish would come true, and I saw a child. He caressed the side of my face with one hand, his touch soft and strong, and with the other, he felt the thunderous beat of my heart. He, in that moment, kept a promise, and I saw a man.

I love you.

I love you.

We had both fought for our lives as children, literally kicking and screaming to get away from monsters. From knife attacks and acts of murder. With vicious reflex, we retaliated with ruthless scratches and hits of our own: pulling hair, kicking where it counts, punching noses, slamming the hand down—our stamp of victory on stunned and stinging and beet red cheeks. Absent, automatic, ruthless control.

We barely existed with ever-present memories of the assault of accusations and belittlements –

You stupid, what's wrong with you

—Wounds deeper than knives and that lurk in dark corners like shadow phantoms, stalking us, waiting to pounce and claw our hearts out. It's the scheming utterances that leave atoms of traumas and tragedies. It's the contorted perceptions and conclusions that linger in currents, suffocating and strangling empty throats with rotted, wasted blood that distracts us from living life.

When we found each other, when he recognized that which is me, and when I recognized that which is he, we defied the damage and death. For a while, we discovered lasting true love.

It's the truth of that moment that echoes for infinity.

I try to remember that when I ask what went wrong. But I know. The shadow phantoms, the looming, greedy, callous beasts, ate their bounty in him, in us. They had spewed doubt in me and in the certain impossibility of dreams coming true. We swallowed those mumblings because we suspected that we didn't deserve purity. We became monsters, attacking, retreating, and retaliating against each other.

The beasts buried pieces of us in cold, suffocating dirt so they could come back and completely devour us later. I saw something far in the horizon before the dirt covered my eyes. A strange, distorted, ugly reflection, but that shone with light, albeit fading. When the beasts left licking our blood from their chops, I gathered what I could and climbed out, shrieking in pain.

I reached back for him, but he looked at me, and I saw something I had never seen before. With glazed eyes, he growled and gnashed his teeth. He grabbed me and yanked me back down. Before I could utter his name, he struck me.

I'll kill you if you leave me

His claws slashed my heart. He strangled me.

Don't leave me here alone I hate you

I looked at his dark, unrecognizable, demonic eyes. I lost my breath. The disbelief collapsed and hollowed my soul into the deep, bottomless hole that is -

I'll kill your daughter

With all my might, the child I had been, wild, impervious, primal, and the mother I was, broken yet capable, I kicked his chest with both my legs and threw him off me. He gasped, his eyeballs protruding like frog's eyes. The air knocked out of him, he choked and coughed. I took the moment to escape.

His shock did not last long. He caught his breath and lunged at me. I kicked his face from the crest of the hole.

I ran for dear life -

Over the hill and through the woods

To Grandfather's house

Alone

I ran into midnight's path. An occasional street light and a few porch lights lit the slumbering neighborhood. The inky black sky seeped between mazes of twisting trees and groaning alleys. The windows of neighborhood houses morphed into malicious effigies defending secrets, gold, and tarts from the likes of me.

It didn't cross my mind to knock on doors to beg for help, because I was in a race. He now chased me from a block away, howling insults, swearing to kill me the moment I stopped or slowed down.

I'll kill you if you don't come here

I knew he would murder me. I ran blindly, anticipating the searing pain that would be worse than when he dragged me in a chokehold, when he beat me as I kneeled before him, when he sucked my breast and my life force with savage greed. This time he would kill me, and I was more certain of that than motherhood.

F'ing come back here

I ran, panting, out of breath. Hopeless.

Just when my pounding heart exploded, suddenly, underneath a street light, there sat a wolf, its fur illuminated by the light. An actual wolf! It looked at me with odd recognition. This wolf, real, humongous, breathtaking, in the middle of the hood, stood beautiful, strong, defiant! I couldn't believe it - but it was a real wolf that would chase me and rip my throat open!

I knew, that on that night, I would die an absolute death one way or another despite my desperate yearning for my sweet little three-year-old girl, despite my own hunger for life. I had no cards, except for one. The way I would die. Would I let the wolf kill me that instant, or would I run back to the man I love and let him murder me?

A tear fell from my eye - for him - memories of his eyes in kindness, of his sweet caress, his thoughtful words. Now lost forever to the beasts. He killing me would be what would cement him into an eternity of hate. Someone who I cherished: finished. My God.

I would rather die by the wolf than to be murdered by someone I love.

Though brutal, within the circle of life I would die with some kind of dignity. I came to an immediate stop and took a deep breath, careful not to look directly into the wolf's eyes. I awaited its charge and its fangs to pierce my throat.

I took a step. Something magic and powerful happened. On that lonely night, I accepted death, and for the first time in my twenty-seven years of life, I felt peace. I felt light as air.

I dared to look at the wolf and felt a mysterious connection. Its brown golden eyes sent me the unspoken answer that has taken me a lifetime to understand. It began with the whispering wolf

You are part of the universe

Tilting its head, the magnificent being watched over me.

I reached my daughter and held her extra tight. In the early morning hours I dreamed of looking into a pond's reflection of dying and living stars, and saw a wolf stare back at me.

The next day, I looked through the neighborhood, and found no sign of the wolf.

I wonder what the wolf had whispered to him.

Rhonda R.

(Dis)placement

Dis place ain't no home for me, Dis place is ugly and shabby
    and cold during winter

Dis place ain't got no amenities I do not love it here,
except that I hate it—
living on the streets or in a shelter--there.

So, I stay here.

Dis place certainly ain't no home, 'cause a home is in your head,
    you create it with your mind.
It's a feeling that a place gives to you, and that you give
    back to it, too.
You want to walk through the door and have its arms greet you
with the kind of love
that you get from your dog.
Or, you want the warmth of the heat
to envelop you when you cross the threshold, welcoming
    you, saying,
"Sit down. Take a load off. Warm up those bones."

I ain't no Eliza Doolittle,
but I know what she means when she sings that song,
    and I'm changing up the lyrics with only one word:

"All I want is a home somewhere, Far away from the cold night
air, Oh, wouldn't it be loverly."

MARGARET JOHNSON

He

He does not have to duck to go through a doorway;
    He does not have to shower to wash his hair;
He does not need to take off pajamas before he dresses;
    He does not have front teeth to brush;
He does not have to find an enemy to start a fight;
    He does not fight with people his own size;
He does not take off his ball cap while he is inside;
    He does not address women kindly;
He does not avoid four letter words;
He does not change out of soiled work clothes before
    he sits on the couch;
He does not pick up after himself, so discarded beer bottles
    sit everywhere;
He does not choose to tie his own shoes or remove mud
    before going out or coming inside;
He never says, "Thank you!" to anyone; He does not eat
    before drinking;
He does not wash his hands after peeing;
    He does not choose to go to church;
He has trouble getting to sleep;
He does not want to consider his dreams;
    He often chooses to stay in his bed;
He does not wear socks in his shoes;
    He does not smoke - but he chews;
He gets lot when he drives somewhere new;
    He never stops to get directions;
He does not cover his gum or put it in the trash;
    He does not stop with one donut;
He does not keep count of how many beers he had;
    He does not wear underwear;

He does not know how to be fair;
    He really just cannot let himself care;
He needs no comb or brush for this hair;
    He drops the washcloth onto the chair.

How dare you?!
You promised so much. You are a disgrace - liar liar.
You made me your crutch-
    Your burden! Your emotional cripple!
You disgust me - creep.
Why can't you stand on your own two feet?
Instead, you move to defect me - to deprive me of all else
    that I value. You only permit your music to be played.
You forbid any other emotions arrayed.
No classical- No jazz- nothing with my kind of pizzazz.
    No folk, No soul –
No wine – only beers so you can buy your male peers
    even if the rent is in arrears.

SANDRA HERMANS

Meet Denver

Denver lives at the intersection of Past and Future. While she tries to be "modern" and keep up to date on the latest tech and trends, she finds it nearly impossible to part with her older possessions.

Often she just spends time sprucing up and restoring these knick-knacks of culture and history, rather than throwing them out to make room for the new.

They're a part of her, she always says; she can't toss them.

Instead, she finds clever ways to make more space, consummate packrat that she is, or to fit more into less.

She has a mouse problem, but usually she lets them be. Sometimes she even leaves food or bedding scraps out for them. Sometimes though she'll set traps or poison out too. The mice don't trust her.

She tends to dress differently day to day. One day it's a nice suit, the next a flowing skirt and beads, the next a leather jacket and boots, and so on. Often she'll be wearing bits and baubles that jingle and rattle as she walks, and it's not uncommon to see her toting a sleek, shiny modern bag, while otherwise looking like a whimsical traveler. Her friends and neighbors think she looks silly, and will on occasion blame her nonsense on the fact she's recently gotten into herbal medicine.

CHRISTOPHER SAMU

Finding Fairness

Fairness. We all want it. It's a human desire.

My lungs were heavy. Feeling like a fish out of water I couldn't take it anymore, so I called the Ambulance. The paramedics arrived, took my vitals and listened to my lungs.

"Your lungs sound bad, what hospital would you like to go to?" the paramedic asked. I was escorted to the passenger side of the ambulance and directed to sit in the chair next to the stretcher. Inside the ambulance surrounded me with medical equipment, grey metal walls, and with the feeling of being alone.

As I sat waiting patiently to go to the hospital, -alone, the paramedic told me to stand up for a search of my body and personal possessions. As I stood up gasping for air, the paramedics patted me down and turned my pockets inside out and asked me if I had a lighter. The other paramedic was searching my backpack. I was pissed off. The fact that I was short of breath wasn't even a concern. I firmly told them twice to get out of my belongings and they didn't.

I yelled at the paramedics, "Get out of my bags, you have no fucking right to search my stuff!" I was furious.

I lost focus of the fact I was short of breath. Appalled to be quite clear!

Out of nowhere two police officers, one male and a female,

rushed onto the ambulance. The male officer came through the side door and the female came through the back door. My thoughts couldn't comprehend why the police showed up.

Once the police made their presence known, the paramedic told me, "If you don't comply with this search you can get the fuck off this ambulance! We don't know who you are, and we are searching you for our safety!"

I got out of the ambulance. I knew I was being treated differently for being homeless. Those paramedics knew they were dealing with a homeless person when they got the call for service.

I questioned the lawfulness to the police. I invoked the fourth amendment, which provides, "the right of the people to be secure in their persons, houses, papers, and effects, against unreasonable searches and seizures, shall not be violated, and no warrants shall issue, but upon probable cause, supported by oath or affirmation and particularly . . .

They refused to listen. The police agreed with the paramedics.

With every breath I took, a wheezing and a crackling sound came from my lungs. It became more noticeable with every word I spoke. The paramedics and the police showed no sense of urgency for my emergency. The paramedics never offered me a breathing treatment.

The male police officer said that they look after their own out in the streets, and for the paramedic's safety, I needed to comply with the search. They made themselves very clear: unless I complied, I wasn't going to be treated and I was not getting a ride to the hospital.

I believe beyond a reasonable doubt that the actions by the paramedics were based on the fact I was homeless. Before I became homeless I was a Police Officer. I can honestly say that those paramedics would have never behaved that way, if I had been wearing my old shoes. Their main focus was my backpack and my pockets. They did not respond to a call involving a weapon or violence, nor was I unconscious that would invoke "implied consent" to search me for medication and / or identification.

Everyone regardless of social status has a reasonable expectation of privacy.

Instead, I went to the doctor's office the next morning and shortly thereafter to the emergency room. Although I am new to my primary care doctor's office and to the nursing staff there, they never subjected me to a search. I walk in their office with luggage in tow and they never say anything. I am always greeted with kindness and respect.

There are still good people in this world. My doctor and the nursing staff give me a glimmer of hope. Homelessness is not permanent, and it should not be a social sigma. Although I am homeless, I am still a human being. It can only get better from here! This little bump in the road will go away. This too shall pass... This too shall pass!

Kim Grier

World Weavers

It started with a single brick A word you said or didn't say
You taught me to love the people who would hurt me
At no one's expense but mine Searching for answers in all the
wrong places
the wrong hearts

One by one you laid brick after brick, lesson after lesson
You trapped me within these walls of dysfunction.

I was young and vulnerable
And you built the world around me I am left with re-teaching
myself How to reach into fire without being burned

And bring out my own heart still beating.
A phoenix soul
Rising from the ashes you left me in,

Now I am the fire I am the storm
And I will tear down the walls you built

I will create
I am the weaver of my own world

THE DENVER VOICE

COURTNEY E. MORGAN

Introduction
Writing at the *Denver VOICE*

For this workshop, I worked with a group of writers and vendors from Denver's local newspaper for six weeks in the spring of 2018. A group ranging from four to seven writers gathered in he *Voice* office every week to share their stories and voices, and try out new writing techniques and prompts.

The *Denver Voice* is an urban and small business newspaper that provides job and entrepreneurial opportunities for people experiencing homelessness and poverty. In just a short time the group of vendors at the Voice churned out a tremendous sampling of work, built strong bonds of community and support, and repeatedly made each other laugh, cry (with empathy), and laugh some more!

JOHN ALEXANDER

Untitled

I woke up this morning still Fighting the Fact
that I have no Home.

Transient, indigent, I Don't have a key to anything that
I can call my own.

Looking at my shoes, Frowning at my only change of clothes.
I stayed there, I stayed here, where I'll stay
Tonight only God knows.

Hmm, it could Be time for a shave, even a Bath
and some oral hygiene, too.
The Library restroom? No, maybe the Truck Stop over
on 5th Avenue.

Well now I am getting kind of Hungry,
Where I'll eat today we'll have to wait and see.

Yesterday was Breakfast from a Restaurant Dumpster,
Lunch from a Fast Food Dumpster,
and Dinner from a grocery store Dumpster
They were all the same to me.

I will Apply for some more Jobs, stop by
A friend's house, who said they Had some money that
I could Borrow.
I am selling some Plasma and cutting this Lawn,
Thank you, Trust me you'll get it all Back Tomorrow.

Everything today that I Should Do, Will Do or
Can Do is Done.
Since I still have time For, I'll enjoy the Rest of
the Daylight and Take in some sun.

Ahhh, Just Feel the Air. Look at the Squirrels, the
Birds, why even all the Beautiful Women seem to be out.

Hey, Hey, Hey, Romance and sex is something right now,
I can't afford to think about.

Well it is getting cool,
soon it will be Dark and cold again.
Wherever I sleep tonight
I hope is Better than where I slept Last Night,
or Anywhere else I've Been.

But Tonight I'll go to sleep with
The same thought as Every Night Before,
That I'll wake up tomorrow
With a key to my House and be
Homeless, NO MORE!

REA BROWN

The Name is My name

Is not my name yet it is my name but it is their name
or it's our name a least it was his name and her name
yes it will be more named although most are named
but the true fame and the Greatest claim is not how
it came
but that it is us.

Rea Brown

Blank

As he sat in the room of time D-day Darkness
with even the sound crying, the smell of never mind
Like stuffy pine, the taste of bitter dirt, his mind gathers
blackness, his face wet with pie, he was dead already
Dead yet he was about to die the spirits whisper it's a lie
the futures clear the reply . . .
I'm sorry, what was the question again?

A Cyrano de Bergerac Type Letter to His Love

My dear, sweet and beautiful
Rose.
Every day without you is the
worst torture I can endure.
The only way I survive is in
the knowledge that we will be
together again
our hearts beating as one like
a giant bass drum. Telling
everyone that we have the
truest love, the purest love.

When I look into your brown
eyes, true magic is shown
for the world disappears
only we exist, floating
in the space of happiness
I see the pain in your eyes
a lifetime of disappointment
and hurt.

There is nothing that I can
do to fix it or erase it,
I can only be there when you
need comforting and to be
there holding you when the next
catastrophe happens in our lives
I would suffer any fate to protect
you from the world and its cruelties.

As I look into your eyes I
see the pattern of the sun. It
is fitting. Because, Before you
my life was dark as pitch Black
as the Bottom of a mine.
When you came into my life
I saw a sliver of light on my
Horizon. The first light that
I had see in years and the
most Beautiful light that
I have ever seen.

I want to see that light in
your eyes everyday. My day
doesn't start until I see your
smile as my life didn't Begin
until I met you.

My favorite memory is us
on the dance floor. My right
hand at the small of your Back
smiling and talking. When you
got that wicked grin of yours
you whispered in my ear.
I stepped back, taking your left
hand in my right, looking deeply
in your Beautiful Brown eyes.

I put my left hand on your shoulder.
I was rough to begin with, but
soon I learned to follow your lead.
We were Fred & Ginger. By the
time we got to the dip, I would
have never broken out into
laughter if you hadn't reached

down and grabbed my cheek.

That night when I walked you to your door, you kissed me for the first time. As I walked to the street, I told the moon to be jealous for tonight, it wasn't even close to being the most Beautiful thing out this night.

Until our next time.

BRIAN AUGUSTINE

Untitled

I am walking from the darkest caves into a Beautiful day

I've lived in my dark cave,
perfectly happy in my way
of life, doing what is needed
to stumble around, content to
live with the little comforts
I had.

When you strolled into my heart
lights came on.

I wasn't in my cave. I am
now in a beautiful grotto.

JAY JUNO

I Am

I am everything
I am them
I am nothing
I am you
I am

Jay Juno

The Room

I walked down the long pale hallway, my father holding my tiny hand in his large, strong grip. But it wasn't strong now and felt loose like his mind was distracted or detached. The sounds of shoes clicking on the smooth, hard floors echoed as I walked by windows with my father and noticed a large grey statue of Jesus standing below with his arms outreached. I felt emptiness and a sense of being mocked by that statue. My father and I approached a door at last and he opened it for me and we entered.

The hospital room was dark and filled with greyed out colors. A small tree and a couple of plants were in a corner. These plants and trees would go on to become as the mommy plants and the mommy tree. To the right of the room was a bed where a woman was lying and her long, dark hair spread around her head like a halo.

Machines and pumps were clicking, breathing, and beeping with the lights glowing in the dark like Christmas lights outside of a house or a tree. My mother loved decorating for Christmas and enjoyed her collection of ornaments, lights, glasses, plates, and other holiday themed decorations.

The woman in the bed moaned and groaned, a corner of her mouth and one eye drooped. She looked at me and opened her mouth but no words came out. I backed away from her, the woman lying in the hospital bed with the tubes and machines surrounding her. Who was this woman?

"It's okay, mom. She's just scared of you," I heard one of my brothers say.

I backed away from my mother, who was now half-paralyzed from a stroke. I turned away to wrap my arms around my father and bury my face, anything to block out what was in front of me in that hospital room in Nashville in March, 1995.

"The cancer went to her brain," my dad said. I was 9 years old.

War on the Poor

Streaming mockery
Un-announced
denouncement
tongues of froggy
swamps
lashing out
flickering
fuck-er-ee
raping mentalities
of life, love, and
liberty
Blinding
justice
mockery
flashing
Bubbling   fleshing
gaseousout
gaskets now
grieving   hygiene
          odored
rocked babies   non-ordered
stoned   rising
flagellating   not in spirit
looney-tunes   but
shredding   sewages
human lives   boorish
upon   banging
granulated   treading
walls   non-deposited
humping   dasher

dumping
trashing
construing
     terrorism   or
Amnesty   lives
to
the   of
Wicked   indignity
dolleroo

Whee, wee, what   Shoot em up
is this   Heads
farce
of equity   not

Democracy   attached
not now
but   to
ever?
            sovereignty

Facts caught
in sewage
drains

JOHN ALEXANDER

The Byproduct and Side Effects of Homelessness

We have all see people on the street corners walking. Hand made signs stating "Help", "Need Help", "Anything Helps", etc., or many of us have experienced direct contact with a panhandler asking for your spare change, while following you as he explains to you why he needs your spare change more than you do.

Every day we seem homeless people loitering in the parks, sleeping on the benches at the bus stops, hanging around down town or the corner liquor store. None of these people seem to have jobs, nor do they seem to be looking for one . The most we, our society, see them actively doing is digging gin dumpsters, loitering, moving around aimlessly, buying dope, getting drunk, waving signs, asking for money (free), passed out on the streets drunk or asleep.

People of our society say these homeless people are all no good. All homeless people are lazy and no count. They are a bunch of alcoholics and drug addicts. They have never had anything in life. They don't want nothing and they will never have anything. Homeless people are not worth mentioning. They will never be worth speaking about and they will never be or do anything in their lives worth mentioning ever again. The most popular belief is that homeless people choose to live this way.

I say none of these beliefs are true. Every year all over the world we have dinner with each other. Wish each other best wishes, spend great happy moments with family and friends. Most of all during this day, we celebrate the birthday of the most famous homeless person that ever lived, Jesus Christ. All of my life, I have know characters from movies, books, fables, spiritual stories (the Bible) and people from real life, past and present.

Most of the characters that I have known have all experienced being homeless. Jesus, Mary, and Joseph. The children of Israel, me, John Alexander, the writer of this article. The Three Little Pigs and more. None of these characters chose to live homeless. None of them were lazy shiftless alcoholics and drug addicts. The characters were not only worth mentioning, they were talked about during their lives and have been talked about everyday long after their deaths.

"Well Johnny, then who are homeless people? Where do they come from? How do you become homeless? Can homelessness happen to me?" Yes, becoming homeless can happen to you or anyone. Homeless people are people just like you and me. Homelessness is created when anyone in a situation comes face to face with circumstances beyond their control. Mary, Joseph Jesus, the children of Israel, or the Three Little Pigs all experienced living homeless. What did all of these characters have in common? They were all faced with circumstances beyond their control.

When Mary found out she was pregnant with Jesus, she lived in a home that was hers. I am sure like any Happy Mother to be she went about the house making plans for the new arrival. Oh, things like making this room or that space into a nursery for the baby and if they do not have a spare room that was no problem because Joseph was a carpenter.

As we turn a few more pages, we find Joseph and Mary on the road, homeless in some other town. What happened? What were their circumstances that were beyond their control? They were at great risk of being killed because Herod the King had just passed a law stating that anyone two years or younger was to be killed. No arrest, no new charges, no taking into custody. Just kill right then on the spot where they stood. Joseph and Mary had no control over King Herod and his army. There they were in a strange town homeless, living in a barn with the animals, sleeping on the ground. Later giving birth to Jesus on the ground of the same barn.

Moving on from one extreme, Mary and Joseph, to the next extreme, make believe characters. The Three Little Pigs. Now these guys had money and/or good credit because each of them had their homes custom designed, built, and with the material of their choice. It does not matter if one little pig wanted his home built with straw and hay, or the other little pig wanted his home built with popsicle sticks, matchsticks, and toothpicks, that was their business. That's what they wanted and they were paying for it.

Now the first little pig was at home, with food in the oven, watching Oprah and folding some clothes that were just taken out of his brand new dryer. When came a knock at the door .A violent knock followed with horrible threats and things, like some huffin' and puffin' and blowing the whole house down. Well the next thing you know, the little pig rushes out the back door seeking safety and shelter because he does not have a home no more.

So, he headed over to his friend's house, the one built with straw and hay. No sooner than he gets to his friend's house, all frightened and out of breath, before he could explain! There is the same knock and the same violent threats. Both little pigs rushed out the back way as fast as they could over to their friend's house built of bricks. Now we have so far two little pigs, homeless. What were the circumstances beyond their control? The big, bad wolf running around the neighborhoods, huffin' and puffin' and blowing peoples' houses down for no good reason.

Show me a person that is homeless and I will show you a person that was faced with circumstances beyond their control. Some of us will still say, "But Johnny, I see people in the dumpsters, panhandling and waving signs, etc." I have personally given people money and watched them go straight to the liquor store and buy dope."

Yes, and this is sometimes true. But what you are really looking at is the side effect and the byproduct of being homeless. You are looking at a person that has become complacent. They have given up, given in, and have surrendered to the situation he/she is in. He has entered the world of homelessness and has not been able to find a way out. He has lost all hope.

How does a homeless person living on the streets feel that he can solve the problem of homelessness when experts and government leaders are throwing up both hands saying, "We don't know what to do." From the Presidents on down, our leaders are saying things are bad, and they are going to get worse before they get better.

Tomorrow, when you see a homeless person panhandling, getting drunk, buying dope, sleeping or passed out on the streets, remember you are looking at the effect and the byproduct of being homeless. What is the final product? You are looking at a person who is homeless and hopeless. This is the beginning of the final product. What does a person who is hopeless and homeless learn? Many people in this situation turn to the use of drugs, alcohol, and suicide.

There are three main stages a person may experience when entering the world of homelessness. The first stage is the shock of losing your home and possessions, and your way of life. The second stage is finding yourself out on the streets. For many people, the streets are very frightening, especially when you can see no end to the cold, dark, unfriendly night. The days are not much better. The days are just a new beginning to the nights. Every situation is new, but most of all strange. Rather you are in an alley, down by the railroad tracks, over by the river or a shelter for the night, standing in line to get a bed to sleep in.

Then there is the third stage. Sometimes the third stage is the final stage, drugs and alcohol. What are drugs and alcohol? Drugs and alcohol are mind, mood-altering chemicals. What is the purpose of these chemicals? The purpose of these chemicals is to help you cope with reality or to help you escape. A homeless person's reality is trying to cope with or escape from their reality. The third stage is also very deceiving because turning to drugs and alcohol is opening the door to drug addiction and alcoholism.

THE WRITE AGE—
DECKER PUBLIC LIBRARY

RAY KEMBLE

Introduction
The Write Age—Decker Public Library

The Write Age—Decker Public Library is a workshop for seniors with an urge to express themselves in language. Every Friday for two hours, senior writers of all skill levels meet at the Decker Branch Library in Denver's Platt Park neighborhood to talk about the craft of writing, to be given writing prompts, to freewrite to the prompts, and to share with other Write Agers what they've written. Often stories are life-memories, often they're short stories, poems, or essays. Write Age organizers Mell McDonnell and I, members of Lighthouse Writers Workshop, have guided the Friday meetings since January 2016. The selections in this volume are the work of Decker Library's Write Age participants.

Joanne Kuemmerlin

VAGRANCY LAWS

A Response to the Actions of the Police and City Officials of Denver
Do not
stand, sit, lie, or sleep on, or in any way whatsoever block, any portion of
any public sidewalk.

Do not
display, set, or leave any personal belongings or any sort of property
whatsoever on any public sidewalk or along any public thoroughfare.

Do not
sit, lie, or sleep on any public or private bench whatsoever;
sit, lie, or sleep behind any public or private bench whatsoever;
sit, lie, or sleep under any public or private bench whatsoever.

Do not
seek shelter in any public park;
seek shelter in, on, or under any public monument or structure;
seek shelter near, beside, or in any public building whatsoever.

Do not
set up any form of impermanent shelter;
seek shelter in any doorway or alleyway;
seek shelter on or under any stairs;
seek shelter in, behind, under, or near any vacant or abandoned structure
whatsoever.

Do not
pick up any food, clothing or other discarded items whatsoever from any
alley or any street either for your own use or that of others;

take any food, clothing or other discarded items whatsoever out of
any garbage can either for your own use or that of others;
take any food, clothing or other discarded items whatsoever out of any
dumpster either for your own use or that of others.

Do not be abused.
Do not be sick.
Do not be abandoned.
Do not be poor.
Do not be laid off.
Do not be homeless.

Do not
take drugs or use alcohol to dull the daily pain, loneliness, uncertainty, or
fear.

Do not inconvenience the people of our good city.
Do not disturb the people of our good city.
Do not in any way whatsoever offend the people of our good city.

Do not ask anything of the people of our good city.

Do not be "vulgar."

Do not be vocal.

Do not be visible.

Do not …
be.

SARA FRANCES

Haiku

Blue bicycle waits
Spring rain drips tiny mirrors.
Cherry blossoms blush.

JOANNE KUEMMERLIN

Thirteen Ways of Looking at East Colfax

An Urban Homage to Wallace Stevens
I. In middle of street,
pigeon stands, looking left, right.
"Waiting for bus, too?"

II. Voucher's all used up.
Someone else gets room; the bugs
get brand new neighbors.

III. Easing loneliness –
Small cantinas, markets, shops –
Ways to still touch "home"…
Mexico, El Salvador,
Ethiopia, Bhutan.

IV. Walking up alley,
one leg limps, his head hangs down –
street dog – tired, old.

V. Need fashion lessons?
Know where to get them! Bus stop
filled with East High girls.

VI. Stoops to get penny.
"Sir, do you need change?" she asks.
"No," he says, "just luck."

VII. Two concert venues,
pet spa, specialty cigars,
"Kombucha or chai?"
Bookstore next to indie films –
Some blocks chi chi up the Fax.

.

VIII. Your free clothes don't fit:
Shoes too big, pants too long, the
jacket much too light.
Standing out in winter wind–
No one will invite *you* in.

IX. Fast food. Doughnuts. God.
Drugs. Sex. Ink. Weed. Booze ... Power.
Stroll the 'Fax – pick fix.

X. Standing in a row ...
Hoodies pulled forward like cowls ...
Strange street corner monks.

XI. Civic Center plan –
Remove benches – "vagrants" leave.
"Urban Renewal."
Oops! You all forgot one thing!
Guess what?! Sidewalk is still there.

XII. Trudging past that church,
Though he's homeless, though he's sick ...
Still makes sign of cross.

XIII. It's true what they say,
"Ain't no rules on the street." 'Fax
violets grow where they want!!!

JOANNE KUEMMERLIN

YELLOW

When I was six
I decided
I would eat
only yellow food.

Yellow
because
it had to be sunny food –
bright and bursting with bangs of flavor!
Chewy yellow gumdrops, crunchy yellow Lifesavers,
and the sharp, sweet tang in the velvety smoothness
of my grandmother's lemon meringue pie.

Yellow
because
I wanted to eat food saturated with color –
macaroni and cheese, butter and mustard filled deviled eggs, .
and
the messiness of the
always, almost-too-ripe,
juice dripping,
August nectarines.

Yellow
because
it had to be incandescent food …
shimmering, glowing yellow food –
pineapple sherbet, lemon popsicles, Duffy's lemon soda and
snow ice cream
made with sugar and eggs.

Yellow
because
I wanted radiance –
the radiance of yellow dyed roses,
those roses always too sweet, too sticky,
those roses on tops of birthday cakes,
surrounded always by green and pink and purple ribbons
    … and balloons.

And yellow
because
I wanted to consume soft,
but luminous, yellows;
the soft, silken yellow
of bananas and creamy puddings,
and the smooth pale yellowness
of the all-too-infrequent
summer salt water taffy.

"Yellow food
is
healthy,"
They told us
in my first grade tour of the grocery store.
"That is why you should eat it –
corn and beans and peppers and squash."

Well …
what did they know of beauty?
They were grownups.
They had lost the magic.

What did they remember
of the sunny and saturated, incandescent and shimmering,
radiant, gleaming,
silken and glowing
luminousness
of
yellow?

PHILLIP HOYLE

A Child's View of Time

When my daughter Desma was around six years old, she loved looking at the baby book her mother Myrna made her. It included a copy of her Birth Certificate with her tiny footprints, health records, jotted memories, a swatch of her curly blond hair, other mementos, and photos galore. Desma always began at the end of the book and worked her way to the beginning. One day I sat with her on the living room couch in our Fort Worth, Texas, apartment as she, pointing at particular pictures, told me stories about her life. When we saw the smiling photo of our friend Jim in a white sweater, she said, "My Black Santa Claus."

My wife had met Jim, a tall, single man, a commissioned officer and M.D. at Carswell Air Force Base Hospital, when he became a customer of hers at the restaurant where she worked. I met him, too, and enjoyed our talks about philosophy, theology, and music. On Christmas Eve he called me asking, "Mr. Hoyle," (I think his formality came from nerves, perhaps afraid of being misunderstood) "could I bring over some toys for your children?"

A single man wanting to do last minute shopping for children on Christmas Eve made sense to me. I said, "Sure. We'd appreciate that." And it was true. Since I was in graduate seminary full-time while working halftime at a church, Christmas was going to be rather spare. Within a couple of hours Jim knocked at the door and to the great delight of the kids delivered big presents wrapped in holiday paper and bows. Since that Christmas he had flooded the kids with presents and friendship.

With a big smile after a couple of page turns, Desma pointed to a photo of herself at age three sporting the little-girl ruffle-rumble panties she had insisted on wearing one summer evening in Wichita, Kansas. She knew our friends Earl and Sue were coming over for dinner. Seated in the living room talking with Earl, I heard her giggling as she descended the stairs from her bedroom looking through the rungs to see just where Earl was sitting. She nervously approached him, suddenly scolded, "Don't chase me," then screaming and laughing ran from the room. I don't recall whether Earl actually chased her or not, but Myrna grabbed the camera and took pictures.

Desma turned more pages toward the beginning of the album, then stopped to show me just how pretty she was as a tiny baby sleeping in a blanket on her Grandpa's lap. He was holding her gently in the big oak rocking chair. "That's Grandpa Vance," she smiled. "When are we going to the farm to see him?"

"We're going in August, just about two months from now." Finally, Desma studied the last page of the book (actually the first) with her baby photo, birth certificate, and that curl of her hair, then closed the volume and looked up at me. "Daddy," she said, "when I wasn't nothin', then I wasn't nothin'." She seemed fascinated with the idea. I knew I was sitting with a philosopher.

ANU RAO

Yes, I Am Who I Am!

It was August of 1994.

She was wearing a long colorful Indian cotton skirt and a matching blouse to go with that. Black beads hung on her elongated neck. Her fair complexion and untamed curly reddish hair gave away that she was from the western world. She looked about twenty-four. She was also headed west in that train, in the summer heat of India. She was quiet and kept to herself. Just to break the barrier of silence which existed in between those tightly placed seating arrangement of that air-conditioned train cabin, I struck a conversation with her.

"Are you visiting India?"

I did not receive an answer from her, but rather a stare! It seemed like her tilted head was still trying to put two puzzle pieces together. Finally she blurted out in her British accent "You speak with an accent, an American accent!" I looked so Indian in my Indian outfit. Yet, the words came from my mouth sounded so American to her. She could not place me in any one place on this earth; she was forcing two puzzle pieces together, which she thought did not belong together.

That stranger reflected my own sentiment!

My life must have been in fast forward last 21 years. Before I realized I had spent half of my life in America as I did in India. I really did not know any more "who I really was."

Am I an American; or an Indian?

Am I an Indian with American influence or an American with Indian traits?

When am I really me? When I wear the western outfits or when I drape myself in Indian *saris*?

For many I encountered, I was neither an Indian nor an American. I was simply somebody who spoke with an accent. Some were polite and complimented my 'interesting' accent. Others ignored me; it was too hard for them to digest the words that stalled from my mouth. Many were lost for words they did not know where to take the conversation. Either I looked or sounded so foreign to them. Either I behaved so foreign or my thoughts were so foreign. Few felt I was from a world beyond their imagination. But, one thing they all agreed that I spoke with an accent; but could not agree if I spoke with an Indian accent or an American accent.

Whenever I visited India, even in my Indian outfit, they could smell a foreign blood. They could hear an accent even in the way my body spoke. It was nothing new for me. I have been accused of speaking with an accent since the time I was born. I wonder, as a baby, if I cried with an accent too! I guess the farther you remove yourself from your native soil, the more you will be indicted of sounding with an accent.

Growing up in India, when I spoke in 'Tamil' at school or with friends I was accused of 'Kannada' accentuation. When I spoke at home with my extended family in 'Kannada', I was ridiculed for speaking with Tamil accentuation. Now, when I speak in English I get indicted of either an Indian accent or an American accent, depending upon the soil I stand on. How is that possible I speak with two different accents?

I suppose, 'accent' is really in the ear of the beholder.

Am I really a misplaced piece of a puzzle? "Who am I?" I inquired myself as the train picked up its speed.

"Am I an Indian? Yes. I am an Indian."

If so, what made me an Indian?

"Was that my genes that I was born with, or the religion I was born into, my childhood, or the Indian outfits I wore? Or was that the sumptuous food that I relished, the Bollywood movies I watched, the games I played, the leaders I adored, the heroes that I had crush on? Or the festivities we celebrated or the little customs we followed in India?" I queried myself.

What made me an Indian, an amalgamation of all of the above?

"What am I saying? The Indian food that I consumed, the movies I watched the games I played defines who I am, today?"

"No, but the memories and experiences associated with all of above constitutes me." I told myself. So, am I saying I am an Indian, even though I have lived in America longer than I have lived in India?

"No," I told myself, "I am an American too."

"Really, what make me an American?"

"Is that my American citizenship or the jobs I have held, my adult life, my new friends in America or the western outfits I wear? Or is that the food I eat, the stories I read, the movies I see, the games I play, the leaders I adore, the talk-shows and the game-shows that blast through my radio and television? Or is that my colleagues, teachers, my American born kids, my experiences, and the places I visit, or the Chevrolet we own? Or are the western holidays we celebrate or the little traditions we have formed?" I questioned.

Yes, I am an amalgamation of all of the above. I am a squirt of Indian and a squirt of American; and some more!

What is that some more?

Whatever that I had ever seen
Even images that I have never seen
Regardless of their precision,
I am the reflection of those images.

Whatever that I had ever heard

Even sounds that I have never heard
Regardless of their clarity,
I am the echo of those sounds.

Whatever that I had ever smelled
Even scents that I have never smelled
Regardless of their redolence
I am the vapor of those scents.

Whatever that I had ever said
Even thoughts that I have never said
Regardless of their wisdom
I am the expression of those thoughts.

Whatever that I had ever touched
Even factors that I have never touched
Regardless of their propensity
I am the replication of those factors.

Whatever that I had ever sensed,
Even spirits that I have never sensed,
Regardless of their vitality,
I am the soul of those spirits.

That train moved fast, in its rhythmic fashion. Yet, amidst
hundreds of people, that train provided me a quiet place of my
very own. In that place of anonymity, I realized, "I am the soul
of my spirits that is who I am."

I am who I am.

I am the smart and the dense
I am the fair and the dark
I am the fun and the drag
I am the good and the bad
Yes, I am who I am.

I might be the wisdom
Yet lack the wisdom for good judgments.
I might be the talent
Yet lack the talent for numinous enrichment.
I might be the power
Yet lack the power for deliberate submission.
I might be the strength
Yet lack the strength for will power.

I am who I am
Solemnly I wait for tomorrow.

Tomorrow a new day will start all afresh!
But for this moment, I remain simply me!
Yes, I am who I am.

Kathy Massman

The Best Ice Cream

It is so hot and humid I can hardly breathe; the sweet-smelling air thick with moisture and the buzz of insects; a typical summer day in the Midwest. It's like a mini family reunion at the farm. Assorted aunts, uncles and cousins are here for the day, in what we kids consider our own private Disneyland; there are cows and chickens to feed, kittens to pet and trees to climb; it doesn't get any better than this.

We've had our big evening meal and our moms have donned their aprons, catching up on the latest family news as they wash, dry and put away all the dishes and leftovers. Our dads are sitting outside in lawn chairs discussing gas mileage, their low voices a hum in the background, as we play tag in the yard.

At days end we are tired, sweaty and covered in mosquito bites, watching the sun go down, listening to the cicadas sing and waiting for the lightening bugs appear. Soon, the sky is full of them and we catch as many as we can and ask for something to collect them in; the bugs looking like tiny lighthouses blinking on and off through the glass of our peanut butter and mayonnaise jars.

We flop onto the cool grass mesmerized by this miracle of nature, trying to figure out how they do it, our energy spent; winding down like old clocks. We are in a dreamy state, the long hot day almost over.

At last, it's time for dessert; our favorite—homemade ice cream!

Aunt May has washed the canister, paddle, and lid for the ice cream freezer, mixed the vanilla, eggs, sugar, fresh milk and heavy cream in a large bowl, and filled the canister to the top, ready to go. While our mothers set out a stack of bowls, spoons, and toppings on the kitchen table, Uncle Albert slips a huge chunk of ice into a gunny sack and crushes it into smaller pieces by pounding on it with the side of an axe.

He packs the crushed ice into the wooden bucket, around the round metal canister with its sweet creamy contents, alternating layers of ice with handfuls of rock salt; adding a cup of water to help the ice melt, settle and shorten the freezing time. Once the bucket is full he snaps down the cranking mechanism over the stem of the paddle and locks it in place with a thumb latch over the prong on the bucket frame. We each take our turn at cranking. Around and around we turn the handle—for what seems like hours—until our skinny little arms ache, then the next cousin in line steps up to continue the task. We watch the canister spin, the melting ice and salt making a slushing sound as one by one we turn the handle for as long as our arms hold out.

As the concoction begins to freeze and the cranking gets harder, one of our dads takes over and continues until the handle will barely move.

The cranking mechanism is unlatched and the lid of the canister is wiped clear of ice and salt so none gets into the ice cream when the canister is removed and the top opened. The bucket is covered with a damp tea towel and left to harden while we bring out the spoons, bowls and toppings from the kitchen.

At last it's time to eat! We line up and Aunt May fills our bowls as we glob on chocolate syrup, strawberry and pineapple sauce, and crushed nuts.

I marvel at the colorful concoction. No dessert in the world could be more delicious than this. We gobble the first few bites until one by one, we are stricken with severe brain freeze; moaning until it passes leaving a thick coating of cream on the roofs of our mouths. Such sweet pain! We stuff ourselves and scrape the bowls clean then ask for second helpings. We continue to eat until the canister is empty and we feel sick from the sugar overload. We look at each other and laugh, this would make a funny group photo; except for our ages, we look identical, each of us with a ring of chocolate around our mouths, a testimony of silent 'O's', as witness to this sweet summer delight.

CHRISTINE HAMILTON-PENNELL

A Day in Totolapan

We drive our van of relief supplies slowly down the narrow streets of Totolapan. At least one house or business on every block is missing walls or has totally collapsed into a pile of bricks and twisted metal. What began as an education immersion experience for my husband Bob and me has taken on an added dimension. On this bright sunny day in November, we accompany our Cuernavaca hosts, Gerardo, Sofía and five members of their family, on their weekly visit to deliver needed supplies to the villagers. Totolapan, like many other villages in central Mexico, was heavily damaged by a powerful earthquake and aftershocks in September 2017.

Next to the town plaza, the ancient cathedral—the center of village life for more than 400 years—no longer has a roof. Part of the belfry and walls have crumbled. The town residents have set up folding chairs under a canopy in the plaza to hold mass. As we learn throughout the day, the villagers' faith provides them with both a sense of hope and community in the face of sometimes desperate circumstances.

Continuing our drive, heaps of rocks still block some of the streets, more than seven weeks after the quake. Luís carefully maneuvers our van around the obstacles. We see men of all ages toiling in the sun with shovels and wheelbarrows to clear away the debris from many of the damaged properties. We hear the persistent honking of young men on motorbikes selling fresh tortillas from milk crates strapped on back.

We stop at one property where a hand-lettered sign proclaims the obvious: "Casa Afectiva." The only thing left standing on the lot is the brick outhouse, a beacon in the midst of a sea of debris. A broken white ceramic toilet lies unceremoniously on its side in a pile of dirt and rocks nearby. A small but hardy squash plant has tenaciously established itself in the rocky soil there. Gerardo greets the middle-aged homeowner outside the temporary shelter in which he and his wife are living. His face is creased with smiles as he motions toward a palette of cement bags and a pile of gravel on the partially cleared lot, talking to Gerardo about the rebuilding process that is underway.

Across the street, a pile of used clothing spills from a giant fiber sack incongruously marked, "For Peanuts Only." We learn that the clothing was dumped there by an aid group several weeks before. But used clothing is not what the villagers need, and now it lays in a damp, moldering heap. The villagers have more important things to attend to than cleaning up this unwanted garbage. What they really need are blankets for the cool nights and staples such as toilet paper and Pampers.

At one turn in the road, we stop the van, and peer down a steep dirt path to two concrete block dwellings partially hidden by the trees. Acrid smoke from an outdoor wood-burning stove assaults our nostrils as we carefully pick our way down the trail, avoiding a mangy dog and protruding tree roots. Sofía takes a bag of supplies to one of the structures, talking at length to an old woman sitting outside shelling dried beans into a metal bowl.

Meanwhile, Bob, Gerardo and I head to the other dwelling. As we enter the house, I recoil from the stench of urine and see the woman struggling to change the diaper of her severely disabled son, lying on a bed at the back of the room. His name is Armando, and he appears to be unable to do anything for himself or communicate with others. I ask how old he is, and his mother replies by telling me his birthdate in November of 1984. I am stunned to realize he is the same age as our son. She has cared for him for almost 33 years. I struggle to comprehend. My heart goes out to her and I wonder if I could have managed to do what she has done, with no end in sight, year after year.

Armando and his mother live in one large room, the bed at one end and the kitchen at the other. Propane tanks fuel the stove, next to a set of shelves holding brightly colored bowls and a yellow wooden table sporting a red vinyl tablecloth. The concrete floor is painted blue and is crumbling in some spots. Electricity is available, at least intermittently. Gerardo gives the mother a blanket and some other necessities. She tells Gerardo she would love to have a small television so that Armando has something to entertain himself during the day. Gerardo promises to try and find one. She has tears in her eyes as she hugs us and says, "El cielo se multiplique su generosidad"—heaven will multiply your generosity.

Meanwhile, the old woman has enlisted Bob's help to climb a rickety ladder and pick some beans growing on a trellis against the outside wall, pointing to which beans are ready to harvest. The diminutive grandmother's grey-streaked hair is pulled back from her weathered face, and she wears a red sweater and skirt, covered by a burgundy-checked apron. When the beans are harvested, she asks us whether we believe in the Word of God. She exhorts us to read the scriptures so we will be saved from God's judgment, when He will destroy the world by fire. As we prepare to leave, with quiet dignity she insists we take the bag of beans with us.

After visiting several more families, all the supplies we have brought are gone, and we head home. We stop at a roadside taco storefront and eat tacos al pastor in the open air, the succulent pork shaved from a giant layered stack on a cone. As we eat, we talk about the people we have visited and how great the need is. North Americans like to feel "helpful," Gerardo explains, but much of the poverty we encounter in Mexico is systemic. The government and police are corrupt, drug cartels perpetrate massive violence, public infrastructure is crumbling, education and healthcare are inadequate, and the church's pervasive influence on society has resulted in Mexico having the highest teenage pregnancy rate in the world.

In view of these facts, what can we do? I realize that helping a few people, as we did today, is no more than a temporary fix. We can connect with them and learn about their lives and struggles, and share our testimony with those who, like us, are more privileged. We have been blessed with education, healthcare, decent housing, clean water and a comfortable life. The poverty we witnessed is real, but the memories that will stay with me are the smiles of the children, and the hope, resilience and resourcefulness of the people we have met. They get up each day and do what has to be done to take care of their families. At the very least, our privilege reminds us to be grateful for what we have, and to do as much as we can to alleviate the difficulties and suffering of others who have received a very different roll of the dice.

HANNAH SCHECHTER

Elegy in Three Parts

I. Death Came Riding

Death came riding for you,
Without concern for your plans
For the future.
Death claimed you
Without regard for my hopes and desires.
Death came riding for you,
Death claimed you,
On her Harley.

You would have wanted it that way,
Little as I will to admit this,
Much as I'd prefer to be angry at you
For leaving me here,
Alone,
Without you.

Death came riding for you
With no side saddle,
Only room for one,
And Death chose you.

I wouldn't rather be dead myself,
That's not what I mean at all.
I just would rather be with you,
Going wherever we pleased,
On your Harley, not Death's.

Death came riding for you
And I bow my head and weep.
Too soon, Death, too soon.

II. "Make Up A Unique Way To Pay Tribute To Someone After
    She Has Died"

I won't pay tribute to you,
I can't,
Not yet.
You aren't dead for me yet.

Your shy smile still lingers,
Disappears around the corner just as I'm about to catch you.
You're still here, breathing the air next to me,
Warming the space beside me,
Still filling my hunger.

I can't say goodbye yet,
Can't shine you on yet,
Can't say more than Godspeed
Because I don't want you to go.

I don't want to say goodbye,
Don't want to drink a last cup of coffee.
I want to sit by this fire with you,
Talk to you,
Laugh and cry with you.

Come to this fire, love, and say goodbye.

III. Only A Miracle

I.
Summer will come again,
But you won't be here for it.
Summer will come again,
But you are out of time now.
Time has run out on you,
You have escaped it.
You have run out of time.

You have run, out of time,
Into eternity,
Run, faster than time,
But speed is irrelevant without time.
You have become timeless, speedless.

II.
Time has called you daughter,
Time has called you, daughter,
For its own.
Time has claimed you,
cancelled your passport,
Made your driver's license (with the motorcycle endorsement)
Of no more currency than a dead moth.

I don't know how to mark time
Without you;
I despair of it,
Fall into my own timeless pit
Without you.

Without you to count the hours
Till our next meeting,
Without you to add up
The minutes we spend together,
I am lost.
I am clockless in the land of timekeepers.

III.
I am in a sea
So dense with pain
Even the tide cannot swim.
Only drowning remains.
My remains drown in sorrow for you.
Now you are out of reach
I am caught in the undertow of time

Without you to counterweight me.

The lifeguards on this beach look the other way.
They look for people they can save.
I am beyond human aid.
Only a miracle could pluck me from this sea,
Only the miracle of your return,
Of your whisper from where time has left you,
Saying "Live, live."
Whisper, so gently, in my heart, "Live, live."

So I will live, to remember you,
To caress your photograph and say "Live, live."

VIRGINIA C. KENT

The Knitter and the Boxers

My grandmother was an accomplished knitter. Her work was beautiful, filled with color and cables, her skill showcased in intricately patterned masterpieces. Each one was meticulously designed, sewn, knitted, stitched and fitted to the size and temperament of the recipient. Every Christmas my brother, sister and I received new sweaters or matching hats and mittens. Tennis sweaters were in fashion the last year she made them for the three of us.

That Christmas morning, we simultaneously opened beautiful white, V-necked sweaters, with red and blue banding across the hem, along the cuffs and on both sides of the V-neck. The front, back and sleeves were fully cabled unlike today, where sweaters often have them only on the front. It's no easy feat to knit cables correctly and three sweaters, fully cabled were quite an accomplishment even for someone with my grandmother's knitting acumen.

When I surprised her for a Fall visit, I found her sitting in her Queen Anne's chair cursing roundly at the sweater on her needles, tearing out row upon row of knitting. Little did I know that at each point where the cables are twisted, they must be turned into the center of the sweater from each side. As she sipped her Scotch Whisky, she explained the rational for tearing out the rows. As I foolishly commented that no one would notice, Gram strongly informed me she did and that's all that mattered.

My college boyfriend Tom pinned me during my sophomore year in college. My grandmother was so excited at the news, she declared that he deserved a handsome sweater and she would make me one to match. Neither Tom nor I were slim and he was a robust 6'2", so these sweaters required a lot of time and yarn to knit. The yarn came in hanks, often selected at local mills, then weighed, priced and taken home to be rolled into a ball. She had ladder-back chairs in the dining room and a hank was suspended from the tops of chair. One would stand there for a very long time and patiently wind the yarn into a ball, supervised by Gram, making sure it was wound with just the right tension, not too tight or too loose. It took hours to wind all the red, white and blue yarn needed for each sweater, which gave her ample time to talk with me about my future. I still have my sweater and although it's fuzzy, too big and in need of being cut down, it still gives me a big smile whenever I pull it out.

When Gram heard Tom and had I broken up during my senior year, she became worried that she wouldn't live to see her great grandchildren. She then began a campaign to knit me a complete receiving set for my unborn, nor even thought of, children. There were yellow receiving blankets of various stitches, hats with chin ties, booties in yellow, pink and blue and little mittens made out of soft baby yarn on very fine needles.

My children, the first who was born over 17 years after Gram proudly gave me the box of knit goods, were wrapped in the blankets with the hats and booties to match. Now stained and pulled, they remain in her 1917 hope chest, which resides in my guest bedroom, hopefully to be worn by any grandchildren I might be graced with.

Her last hand knit gift to me before she put her needles down for good, was a Fair Isle cardigan sweater knit on one round needle from the hem to the collar. The sleeves were knit on separate round needles and once completed, were joined to the body of the sweater at the shoulder on the larger round needle. The neck was completed and the sweater finished. As she gave me the sweater, my grandmother told me that because the pattern was in French, she had to figure out the Fair Isle pattern as she knitted. The sweater ended up being enormous as her French was limited. No matter, it was beautiful and long enough allowing me to cover the weight I'd gained in college.

Mittens were her signature piece. Over the years, she made all of the family, friends, co-workers and who knows how many others, mittens. Pairs and pairs of mittens in various sizes and colors but always in the same pattern with a single cable down the top of each mitten. Each pair was knit on a set of very long needles at the same time with separate balls of yarn, so they would finish with identical lengths. They were made specifically for each person with proper length of the hand and thumb areas with a long, snug cuff to fit up your jacket sleeve and keep the snow and cold out.

My petite, blue haired, blue blooded Bostonian grandmother loved watching boxing. Those strong hands on half-dressed men, slashing through the air smacking flesh with a loud thunk, blood spinning in threads from cuts lips, entertained her for years on cold Friday nights in rural Vermont. Her living room was out of a Currier and Ives Christmas card with a roaring maple log fire warming and giving the air outside and in her home the unmistakable perfume of Vermont winters. The small TV rested on a table in a corner by the fire and Gram would have to sit forward and squint to watch the fighters roam around the ring. As she closely followed the fight's progress, the clack of her needles mimicked the speed of the fight. The mittens forming on her needles swung freely like the boxers gloves as they moved toward their target. She would sigh when the match was completed, commenting on the boxers and count stitches sipping a wee bit of whisky before the next match began. She continued to knit mittens and watch the Friday night fights until she no longer could do either. I taught her to crochet in her 70's when her hands became less agile because of age and arthritis. This allowed her to have fun making baby blankets, lap rugs and bed spreads with one hook rather than two needles.

I still have and wear the last two pairs she made for me, but sadly the thumbs have worn out. "A stitch in time" is wise advice, which I didn't heed and now am trying to repair the damage. I have a skein of bright red worsted wool left over from another mending project, which I'm using to rebuild the missing parts of each thumb. When these repairs are done and the red patched thumbs keeping me warm, I will keep all these memories of her close to me once again.

Sara Frances

A Love Story with
Hardware Inclusions

It was years later, looking back, that she ascribed the success of her second marriage - indeed the alarming leap of faith entailed in getting married again, and exultantly to the man she had hoped to marry as a teenager - to her heated garage.

As a child she loved the deep forest of hardware stores. Who needed the bright lights and plastic colors of toy emporiums when you could get lost in drab and crowded aisles, bins of nails and screws of undefined purpose, downspouts and toilets, tools, light bulbs, faucets and electrical cords? Sheer numbers of tiny items, interspersed with dish towels picturing embroidered chickens and much anticipated Santa Claus window stickers, which predictably appeared the moment Halloween masks, sold out. It was a matter of devotion, a religious experience. One year she strapped a 20-foot ladder to her VW bug as a Christmas present for her Mother. The gift was well received.

Her tool collection increased with years, exponentially - no surprise - along with partially used cans of paint too valuable to throw out, collections of seeds gathered from neighbor gardens, extension cords by the drawerful, at least a dozen various tape measures, work gloves (thin for light duty and heavy mitts impervious to chemicals). She became a proud homeowner; a proper, attached garage was needed.

It was a design project for adults, ripening into a workshop of everyday life, more important than any ordinary living room. While most living rooms are cold affairs, literally and figuratively, kept embalmed in unexpected-guest-readiness, sterile, neutral, fixed and non-committal, the garage had to be hot with style and purpose, a heart of activity. Vibrating with can-do, what-if spirit. Big, waaay bigger than the living room, lots of exciting cupboards, racks and bins, hooks and drawers. An aluminum garbage can bristling with brooms, rakes and shovels.

And there would be a real industrial sink with water, hot and cold, and a gas heater - a hearth for the home. Drive your car right into your living space, just like in old Mexico. The convenience of never unloading groceries in the dark, cold or wet. An anchor for the ship of organized agglomeration, humming with life.

The man appeared seemingly out of nowhere and everywhere, from the future as well as the past. He drove a lifted red F250 with fat, no-nonsense Hankook tires. A polished yellow trailer towed his welded handiwork toward installation on high-rises, kitchens, oil fields and hotels. Big he-man stuff. He looked the part, acted it too.

She had fallen for him as a 17 year old; she was now 53. Much had passed; much remained the same. Hope and suspicion teetering on a fulcrum of desire. Could she forgive that he had simply disappeared, no word or breakup? Could he disregard that her parents disliked his father intensely? Was there a road back? He had more tools than she, she remarked with some envy. Tools as well kept and organized as hers, perhaps better. He lived the axiom that a new job would green-light the purchase of new and more fascinating equipment.

Months passed. Tentative, unrequited overtures on both sides. Then things went over the top. After one wonderful date, which incidentally included an installation involving a front loader, forklift, crane, dump truck and two 18-wheel flatbed trailers, he didn't leave. What if he left again? Girls need space; getting what you want can be too much, too scary. She kept trying to think how to shoo him out, but "go home" never quite got verbalized.

Then it turned out that he spoke cat; her kitties adopted him immediately, switching dishonorably to his side of the bed. Whisker licking and smug, without remorse. Perhaps it was all ok; cats know these things. He gravitated possessively to the garage. He took up car detailing, necessitating a bigger DeWalt air compressor, power washer and Master Blaster among other fancies.

He moved in with three red tool cribs and the truck. If you stop by, don't bother coming to the front door; come to the alley; we'll be in the garage.

Ruthie Urman

Table Talk

they sit at the kitchen table, on our 50s white with black
speckles linoleum tile floor, surrounded by bright yellow
walls, my mother's solemn face, her eyes purposely averting
my father's critical ones, looking down at her hands, wrapped
around the coffee mug; she looks sad, as if she could never
would never will never receive the love she always craved,
always wanted, always humanly deserved, even though she
didn't realize it at the time and perhaps still doesn't understand
the depth, the gravity of not getting enough love; my father sat
on the table's corner from her, deep in his eggs, slurping them,
not quite cooked through, like their marriage . . .

they would talk, my mother's voice low and lacking in any
luster or joy, as if she was already defeated before she began,
her eyebrows raised, as if she was in a play, rather dramatically
and my father, seemingly more interested in his plate before
him, the still slimy over easy eggs, the toast and his coffee. his
coffee breath always put me off; it felt stale and stuck, dry like
his cracked lips, like his emotions and his viewing of me as a
young child, as a teenager and then, mysteriously widened,
as an adult; no longer rolling his belly for the neighbors on
our front porch; eating much less and losing his belly weight
(paunch), that was not too much in the first place.

my parents at the kitchen table.

did they even ever look one another in the eyes? i don't know,
it didn't seem like it or that they even witnessed the other; it
was more like each of them would put on a staged show of
feelings, somewhat dramatic yet dulled down by time and jaded
experiences, individually . . .

my parents at the kitchen table.

as a woman, i can't get enough touch because the only touch i
received was my mother's back scratching as i sat at that same
table, her fingers behind my chair and now my back, like you
have told me, many times, has a million clitorises on it i'm that
sensitive that yearning that wallowing in your touch and my
discomfort when i am ignored or not felt with your fingers....
whether bloody, doused with gasoline from the car or cracking
in winter's dryness . . . i search for your gnarled hands and
fingers, from accidents past.

is our relationship an accident?

my parents at the kitchen table.

so alone with one another

are their hearts as empty as their sex lives must have been? my
mother looks like she wants to cry, like a baby, held by someone
other than her distant, russian mother; the only memory i have
of her is her gifting me with a towel sporting a candy cane—i
did love that towel, even though my Bubby seemed so fragile
that i thought she might break, right then. and that's how i
always thought of her, my stooped over, thin, china cup, Bubby.

i am so lonely with you. you tell me you want to walk together,
yet you never follow me, you are either behind or in front of me
and millions of miles away, in your mind . . .

there you go again, leaving me for your mind

my parents at the kitchen table.

and when we do go out to eat, i spend most of the time by
myself; somewhat embarrassed because i sit waiting for the
food, the waitress and you
    . . . alone at the table, cradling my hot drink, dreaming of

better times; where the fuck did you go? why do you do this?

is my father sipping his eggs to allude my mother's questions, does he care, is he moving in complete fear of her wanting intimacy?

so alone.

my parents at the kitchen table.

my life, mirroring their sadness, aloneness and loneliness.

it's why i can't leave you, at this time; it's because i will be completely alone, adrift, lonely, partnerless . . . yet am i not more alone when i am with you? no answers come, only the unhealthy "ness" of us the unhealthy "ness" of my parents the unhealthy "ness" of loneliness.

my parents at the kitchen table.

CHRISY MOUTSATSOS

The First Time

I finally felt a bit less exhausted, or maybe braver, and I walked into the small bathroom. My arm and chest muscles were still very sore and tight from the surgery. All I could do at this point was to unbutton my pajama top, gingerly open it, and reveal my sore chest.

The white tape covering up the incision stretched from one armpit all the way to the other. The surgeon told me to leave it alone until it fell off by itself.

But patience is not one of my virtues. I picked up the tape from one end and slowly began to peel it off.

The pain did not make me scream, but it certainly gave me pause. "Take deep breaths girl," I remember ordering myself.

The long, red, puffy incision trailed the contrasting thick black markings drawn on my flesh to guide the scalpel. There were no visible stiches, just sore skin glued together.

So, there it was staring back at me in the mirror. The outcome of several months of intense agony, deliberation, and difficult decision-making.

No more middle-age pendulous breasts. No more erect pleasure-seeking nipples. I was completely flat, like an unsuspecting 5-year-old. The only thing the stood out now was my Buddha belly.

I turned off the lights and slowly made my way back to bed.

Jennifer Tawse

Untitled

On road trips with my family when I was a kid we loved snacking to pass the time. I probably ate pounds of Nacho cheese Doritos chips and ice cream sandwiches and those little chocolate chip cookies. I can remember my cheeks were dusted with sugar and cheese bits and my lips looked bright orange. I was cool with that. We always had snacks.

Yesterday, my 52-year-old body forgot to eat dinner as I was with my brother in the hospital. In the ICU at 6 pm you either leave or stay till 8. My brother asked me to go at 730 in a kind voice but I had to stay in his room till 8. I didn't feel hungry. I felt relief that my brother was alive. I have this memory of my brother as a 16 year old on a summer day that I hold in my mind, like a polaroid that I can go back to. He's come back from another day out in the woods with his best friend. There is this large redwood tree to the left of him. He's got a basic white tee shirt on and blue jeans, his hair is Scottish blonde and his skin is golden from the many hours of hunting and hiking. He is smiling and he knows how to live life.

Anyways, I was trying to be quiet in this little room of beeping machines and oxygen tanks when the nurse opened the sliding door to tell my brother that there was family to see him and she knew one of them as she was a respiratory therapist at the hospital but also a dear friend of Rich. "They are firm on coming in Rich. You ok?" Rich smiled and said, "Oh Julie, we go way back". That was Rich saying he knew her from the program but keeping her anonymity. Then three characters came to the sliding door and were waving at Rich and rushed into the room.

An hour before, I could sense that my brother was afraid and confused, so I asked him how he was feeling and he shed a few tears and quietly asked, "What the hell happened to me?" But when these three dear friends surrounded his hospital bed he sat up, reached out to them, and grasped their hands firmly and he wept and wept and looked at each of them with love and gratitude and vulnerability, naked and scared. I could tell they knew each other deeply.

One was a woman who Richard had mentioned to me over the years. She looked 60 and stood like a ballerina with wrinkles and kept combing Rich's leg with, "We love you Rich". The quietest friend was as thin as the cane he leaned on, wore a Harley Davidson Levi jacket and trembled plenty. And the third friend, "Julie" was this smart, stylishly dressed cute 30-something who couldn't stop talking because she couldn't believe Rich was sitting up and awake. She told Rich she had recently been working with Rich when he was asleep and intubated and told him he was on so much oxygen that she worried that he might not make it. "This is my sister, Jenny" Rich kindly said to them.

There were a few pleasantries, but what I mostly remember was the bright woman saying, "Your brother saved my life. I am here because of Rich. Yep, he never gave up on me. I went in and out of recovery and he was my friend." She was sober and now had an amazing job and was thriving. My brother was a huge part of her story and she shared that with me. My brother who forgets to brush his teeth or watches TV instead of getting a job, my bruised brother who never does his laundry or showers and who has a major mental illness helped this bubbling delightful woman?

The older woman simply told me she loved Richard and had been crying all week. I sensed that she was a mother figure to my brother for many years but also there was love and wisdom going both ways between my brother and this graceful woman. There were several comments to me about Rich' big presence in AA meetings in the city.

I thought I was close to my brother. Long ago we were the middle kids in a house full of vodka and despair. I thought I knew all of him. But this tall beautiful messy man saves lives?

Anyways, I said goodbye and got on the highway and felt hungry but it was late and I wanted to get home by 11. My windshield fluid ran out so I stopped to refill that up. I was nervous driving in the rain because my wipers and windshield are useless. At the convenience store I decided snacking would distract me from the future crash that I was sure would take place. I bought 2 Krispy Kreme glazed donuts, two packs of Fig Newtons and a bag of Red Swedish fish. I didn't want soda because that was too sugary (tee hee).

I got in my car and ate the Fig Newtons first. Gag! They were so dry. I remember loving those as a kid but not anymore. Then I started in on the Swedish fish. They were the perfect distraction, small, sweet and chewy and I devoured the whole bag as the storm was relentless. I never ate the donuts, I have my limits. I finally made it home and went straight to bed. At 2 am I felt a rise of those little fishes swimming up my throat and out of my mouth. I ran to the toilet and held on for a half hour. "you are 52 years old, Darlin'. You can't snack like a goddamned teenager, ya fool. And without water for God's sake?" some wise voice said above my head. Nevertheless, as I got up I realized suddenly that I am more than the sum of my mistakes.

Esther Ann Griswold

Whatever Happened to the Rickets Sisters

We were five, plus our military Jewish
father and plump Baptist mother,
living in a Dutch Reformed area,
chased and teased by older neighbor boys,
so we made fun of the Rickets sisters,
because they strutted around
their front yard to Souza music,
twirling and tossing batons,
while their father travelled,
selling encyclopedias.
They in turn laughed
at the people next-door – Mr. Olds
worked as a gas station attendant;
the three children were skinny,
always hungry.

My brother and I spent
countless hours with block kids
our age playing prisoners of war
or Gulag camps in the Olds' dark
two-story house, even though Mrs. Olds
never closed the bathroom door when using
the toilet. When we tired
of concocting torment
and suffering, we held
lackluster tether-ball tournaments
in the Olds' dusty back yard
until dusk or hunger drove us home.

Sometimes we would move
in a herd down the block,

bringing out grim Mrs. Vanderwall, who
threatened to call the police as we walked
on her grass. If we were lucky,
Mr. Plomp, a postman, had left his car
unlocked, and we would rifle through
the mail that littered his back seat,
searching for postcards that said love, or
studying catalogues of people in underwear.
Once, Sharon Vaughn – she lived on the
corner—asked us in to look at her father's
scrapbooks of pornography, but we never
liked her, because she rode horses
and thought our games were silly.

Our family had an upright piano painted white
with ivy decals glued on the front,
and my older sister's boyfriend
played Bach's Two-part Inventions
on it too fast. Three of us took
piano lessons from Joyce Orr,
who had a studio with her bedroom
in the back. Now and then, a man would stand
in the doorway, and Miss Orr would speak sharply
if we looked at him. The middle sister
took tap dance lessons, and our brother's only
lessons were how to be manly
through the Highlander Boys,
but he played the piano by ear.

Now the parents are gone, our brother felled
by cyanide, and the middle sister
dead from cancer. Now we are three,
and we assiduously study
the rules of endgame, the main ones
which are, *no matter what,*

to be defiant, brave and cheerful, and
never look back or question your own life,
although it is alright to wonder
whatever happened to the Rickets sisters.

SHARON NOVY

Writerspace

It is a park for the child in my mind to romp freely. My old adult body takes it there three to four times a week for four to six hours. Its dark green carpeting the grass, its large oak desk the equipment that lets my small body escape to whoop, soar and imagine through the pen held in my hand. It is a rented space in the attic of a mansion; a quiet place to yell onto a page with my language, telling stories at the end of a life well spent.

I've been given the chance to explore music with instruments and performance. I've taken parts to mold characters and release myself to the honesty of the stage. I've drawn and photographed what I have found to be compelling yet something was evading me. Over all the years of work in careers spent caring for and serving others, it is time to serve myself. I am approaching it with the intention of developing a sense of commitment and discipline, bringing a work ethic to a hopeful art form, but the child rushes ahead to capture the moment with abandon and I gratefully sit to watch. This is a weekday venture and the weekends are spent resting my hands and mind to perform the expected duties of the host parent, the maintenance duties of house and home.

The child roars awake on Monday instantaneously invasive and demanding. I indulge its needs with a growing love for its energy, its life force. In reading over some things written, I feel a little inside out with seams and labels showing, a little too sloppily dressed for the public but in acceptable playground attire. I can clean it up later or maybe not. The bumps and scrapes and bruises of this playground should probably be looked at with care. In the comforting eyes of a parent, the child grows to independence.

Wrap Me in a Gown

Oh wrap me in a gown of gauzy teal
    Which smells of oranges and dried lemon peel,
        With emeralds edging neck and hems of sleeves,
           And ribbons echoing the aspen leaves.

Oh wrap my hair in seaweed-colored strands
    With braids made long to cover up my hands.
        Please give my feet two greenly-dyed wide bands
           To rest them on the warming fine-grained sands.

Now lay me on the beach where sunlight shares
    The bay with lapping water shining fair,
        Don't cover up my eyes, but let them see
           The azure sky which always called to me.

        Oh promise me that you will leave me where
        I'll greet new stardust, and return to air.

SARA FRANCES

Haiku

Little man: tough guy
innocent with attitude.
Big Boots soon to fill.

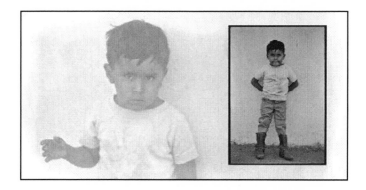

THE VETERANS
AFFAIRS WORKSHOP

Seth Brady Tucker

Introduction
The Veterans Affairs Workshop

I've been lucky enough to be invited to serve Veterans through multiple organizations including nonprofits like the Wounded Warrior Project and Operation Family Caregiver, so when Lighthouse asked if I would like to teach introductory workshops here in Denver, I enthusiastically agreed. I had recently made a promise to myself (and Olivia) however; that I wouldn't take on any more work so that I could give myself over to the needed work for finishing my novel. The thing is, I just cannot say no to anything that has to do with veterans and it gives me such hope that perhaps we are learning once again how to help our warriors to heal.

Of course, my willingness to be a part of this is also likely attributable to my own time in the service, but it is more than that: I love watching these writers begin to chip away at the hard stone of their own buried wells, listen to them read their own work with newfound pride and see their epiphanies, and watch them huddle over a piece of writing in the workshop, the deep spring water rising and then bulging up from the depths, water spilling over and out until this new creative release rises high up over their everyday problems, disabilities, and concerns. I tell all of my students at one time or another that writing is magic; that we are dealing with incantations and spells, and that our language and poems and voices and stories will show the reader a vivid and rich world, filled with real characters and thoughts and stories even when we no longer walk it. It is truly miraculous, and the Lighthouse Veterans Affairs Workshop has shown me how that magic can also heal.

The workshops have been populated by retired colonels, disabled veterans, current National Guard and Reserve soldiers, by Marines and navigators and Special Forces and medics and infantry and mechanics and Navy helicopter pilots. In some cases, the workshop members have been writing for decades and in some cases they have yet to put pen to paper, but for all the workshops there was a sense of brotherhood that is impossible to deny. While sitting around the big mahogany table on the ground floor of the Lighthouse, I was constantly impressed and amazed by the poems and prose coming from these veterans; and I was also humbled by their work as well, not only due to the subjects they wrote about, but for the care with which they handled those subjects. One Navy veteran wrote about cleaning the inside of his helicopter after losing two men from blood-loss. One Army veteran wrote about her standing up to her abusive husband even though that meant she would be homeless. A Marine wrote about his time in Vietnam and the agony and will it took to lift and pull three of his dead compatriots up a muddy embankment in the middle of a firefight, just to have them airlifted out. The thing I remember most about this piece was that he had no sense of the war around him as it happened, that he hoped that maybe he too would be shot and it would finally all be over. To say that I have not had tears in my eyes during these workshops would be the baldest lie I have ever told.

The deployment of any project like this is due to the work of untold others, and it is the same in this case: Dan Manzanares took his vision and made it happen, and Sarah El Hage and Jessie Durham did the heavy lifting of ensuring that those veterans who needed it could get a ride, that our schedule was available, and that each and every veteran in their network heard about us.

Many of these veterans were able to generate material that they submitted to the National Veterans Art Festival each summer, and I get the occasional email from these men and women updating me on the way their new writing habits have changed their lives. I know this feeling: it is the same one I get every time I sit down at my computer and it is the same feeling of release and relief that I felt when I first began to write my little poems in the bottom of a foxhole in Iraq so many decades ago. Many thanks to all the good people at the VA, at Lighthouse, and also to those veterans who have joined me in the workshop: the magic has filled me and changed me too.

D. Glorso

The Major's Mail Call

Like Santa Claus, I drop the sack
Letters from the "World", I sort and stack

Some familiar some new, as I flip through the mass Some
special for Marines, missing or killed in the act

Vietnam, my job, the mail takes care Then I see the letter, scent
fills the air

The handwriting so perfect, the black ink so clear The blue-
green envelope smells sweet and dear

She doesn't yet know, the word just around The Major's
mission, must have met ground

He's the XO, I look up to, all give him respect
I stare long and hard at the letter, and cock my neck

And reflect on the times, I handed him the stack Blue-green on
top, in his chair he'd lean back

His feet found their way, to the crate called his desk With a
smile he'd thank me, I'd deliver the rest

Leaving him to read the letter, scented so sweet Now I wonder
how many years, she will weep

Not knowing the fate, of her man so dear Missing in Action,
must be every love's fear

The cross on the wall, not yet removed The Major's Mail Call,
death not proved

D. Glorso

Marriage – Divorce

It was a wonderful vehicle
At its peak
But a sudden bump
Caused oil to leak

At first the proud couple
Maintained it well
On lookers thought
The ride was swell

But the trickle of oil
Did not seem keen
Just a small mess
A nuisance to clean

Is it the War
They had to pay
Or the forgetfulness
Of a special day

On and on
The years pass
Raise a family
Love the brats

Enough was said
That fateful day
The Valentine's
Won't cuddle hay

Instead they tore up
The ragged pink card
And drove their pride
To the scrapping yard

No parts to salvage
No parts to save
Just drop it in the crusher
And walk away

JIM BISHOP

A Date To Remember:
December 13, 2013

You would think with everything that had happened since the story
("the 6 year old that is trying to save NASA") broke and went viral
worldwide, what could possibly send it viral worldwide again? The
last man who walked on the moon could...he had heard of Connor's
story and called the TV Station asking how he could get in touch
with Connor. He wanted to call Connor and show support for his
cause. The arrangements were made, the meeting would happen on
the 31st, the Anniversary of Gene Cernan's last walk on the moon.

The reporter from the TV station KUSA-TV and Crew showed
up at Connor's house, he
was surprised, as no one had mentioned another interview. The
Reporter who worked well with kids, started asking how everything was going, anything new to tell her etc. When the phone rang
she said "Why don't you answer that?" When Connor said "Hello"
a voice said : "Hello Connor, my name is Gene Cernan, I am an
Astronaut and I was the last man to walk on the moon."Connor's
eyes got big and his smile even bigger. WOAA!!!!

Gene asked if Connor knew of him, Connor responded: "Yes
you were the Flight Commander of Apollo 17 and the 11th and
final person on the moon."

Gene : "Did you know I had a car on the moon?"

Connor "Yes, you had the Moon Rover and while driving you hit a rock and flew through the air."

Gene: "Connor, how do you know so much about me?"

Connor : "I watch Cosmos and I read a lot of books on Space Travel and NASA."

Gene shared with Connor, "I see so much of you in myself, I was the boy who dared to dream of becoming an Astronaut and flying to the Moon. I did it and more." He wanted to encourage Connor to never give up on his dreams even during the trying times NASA currently finds itself in.

Thy talked for quite a while "kindred spirits" with decades between them like they had been friends forever.

Connor asked : "When leaving the moon what was the last thing you saw?"

Gene: "I saw the beautiful world we live in . . . the beautiful Colorado mountains you call home."

Gene: "There's two things you have to do in order to go to the moon. You've got to dream about things that a lot of other people think you can't do. My generation proved that we could make it to the moon and back, it's up to Connor and his generation to take us the next step."

Connor's adventure lasted for a couple more months but that's another story. I will tell you that Connor and Gene did meet each other in person 1 year later at CU Library

Auditorium in Boulder, Colorado where Gene was giving a lecture about his new book. The gray haired gentleman in suit and tie was in good shape for being 80 years and all that he had experienced. He stood tall answering questions about space and his time on the moon. He was to bring Connor up on stage and introduce him and share Connor's story, but time ran out . Connor was very persistent and weaved his way up through the crowd to Gene after the lecture, "Mr. Cernan, my name is Connor Johnson," Gene stopped raised his hands up to the crowd of fans of this living legend. He introduced Connor to the crowd and shared his story, finishing with this : "I dreamt I was going to be an Astronaut and fly to the moon and I did ! Don't ever lose sight of your dream to be an Astronaut and fly to Mars - you will! I just wish I could be there to see it."

This proud Grandpa (Papa Jim) THANKS Gene and all the people associated with NASA-KSC , the totally professional TV news crew that worked with Connor on all the interviews, the World Press for their honest reporting of Connor and NASA to the world. A special thanks to family, friends and supporters that helped take this simple opportunity to teach a young boy about the Democratic process and turning this experience into the more important lesson and inspiration of paying it forward to the next generation.

Never give up on your dreams!

WRITING TO BE FREE

Joy Roulier Sawyer

Introduction
Writing to Be Free

"I write myself out of nightmares and into my dreams," says Terry Tempest Williams, in her essay *Why I Write*. "I write to the questions that shatter my sleep."

More than a year and half ago, Lighthouse Writers and the Jefferson County Public Library launched Writing to Be Free, a collaborative writing workshop serving women in a Colorado facility who are transitioning out of prison.

These writers want freedom from inner demons, freedom from shattering questions. And they also want the freedom to write truthful stories—to join with other women in our culture who, like Williams, also write their way out of nightmares and into better dreams.

On every 1st and 3rd Thursday of the month, JCPL librarian Cecilia LaFrance and I offer this co-sponsored writing workshop for incarcerated women at the facility. On the 2nd and 4th Thursdays, Cecilia visits the center with the JCPL bookmobile, where she fields book requests, hunts down favorite movies and magazines, or handpicks young adult novels she knows the women will enjoy.

She also encourages them to use the library's many resources, including job help and literacy programs for their children. To these women, Cecilia is more than a visiting librarian; she's a trusted friend.

Our bimonthly writing workshop might include reading an excerpt from Jeannette Walls's *The Glass Castle*, or a Mary Oliver or Maya Angelou poem. The participants write in response, share personal stories, offer positive feedback.

Most recently, we read aloud a poem by Jimmy Santiago Baca, "I Am Offering this Poem," then discussed his inspiring story. Baca was violent, illiterate, and serving time in prison on a drug charge when a caring man began to write him letters and send him books. Using a dictionary, the poet painstakingly read and responded to his correspondent. He later became a well-known poet, memoirist, and screenwriter.

Because of our hopeful conversation about Baca's life, as well as discussing the importance of letter-writing, the women struck up a meaningful correspondence with the Hard Times Writing Workshop. Like Baca, the women at the facility experienced first-hand how writing and receiving letters could not only hone their writing skills—it could be life-changing.

The women in the "Writing to be Free" workshop often write about the dreams they have for after they're released, which for many includes more writing. Since the Hard Times Writing Workshop has encouraged the women to join us after they leave the facility, many are dreaming of the day when they're welcomed for good into our weekly Arvada workshop.

At our bimonthly gathering, usually every participant voluntarily shares her work. These women love to write poetry and rhyme, or even songs. Some draw up their courage, take a deep breath, then bravely sing for us.

In many ways, these women have less to unlearn than a lot of writers; they write their way into the heart of a matter very quickly. No posturing, no beating around the bush, no hiding behind masks.

"Everything in here is face value," writes one regular participant. "Coming here means you're for real."

Another writes: "I enjoy this workshop because it allows me to share pieces of myself that I feel others should know. I journal daily and in a way, I hope that someday someone will read it and understand me better. Leave my story behind, so to speak. I think writing our stories benefits a lot of women here."

There's only one aspect of this workshop for which Cecilia and I were entirely unprepared: the gratitude these women express. They thank us profusely every time we visit: for the writing exercises, the journals and pens, the books and films, the fresh bananas and grapes and granola bars, for interrupting our lives to come see them.

During one of my most recent visits, a writer thanked me for bringing soft napkins, not paper towels. It means so much, she said. The human touch. The little things.

I wept.

We are all writing to be free, I said.

In Praise of the Things That Make Me Feel Less Lonely

There is always spending time
with my son, and a person
I'm in relationship with.

Yes, my kids will always be
my beautiful sunshine, too.

I like being around sober women,
loving my freedom, and my son's
sweet innocence.

I feel less lonely reading and studying
the Bible, and having humility—you know,
to go talk to someone when they're down.

Oh, yes, I think getting closer to God—
with God all things are possible.

If I break away from negativity, I'm
less lonely. I've learned the opposite of
selfishness is selflessness.

I'll tell you a few: music, friendship,
writing, sleeping, searching for happiness
in the vending machine, looking in the mirror,
casting out my fears, reminding myself that
it's OK to share my tears.

I like diversity, the boldness of being.
When it's not there, it's like just one
person talking in a room. I'm Mexican,
and my mom told me once that people
will always treat me differently. So sad.

This might sound strange, but
here's one last thing that helps me
feel less lonely: going to Disneyland
and letting loose, feeling like a kid
again.

These are the things we praise as
the women of ICCS—the things that
help us all feel less lonely.

And we wrote this poem
together.

Women's Correctional Facility Group Poem

Precious as Her, and Desperate as Me

from the title of a poem by Theresa W. in Poems from the Inside,
a collection from the Hennepin County Adult Corrections Facility

Warm sensations,
and a peace I can't understand.

An angel sent; a kiss on the cheek.
I think I can see the glow in her eyes.

I can see the preciousness inside:
the person that's awesome,
not the person that's weak.

Precious as her, and desperate as me.

What's desperate? I'll tell you:
desperate is peeing in a cup
in front of a stranger.

And me—I'm trying not to wade into
the desperation, the desperation
of the unknown.

Precious as her, and desperate as me.

I'm still trying to figure out what's precious.
The woman inside sees innocence in me.

Maybe now I might belong to myself,
no one else. Belong to no one
but me.

Yes, precious as her, and desperate as me.

AUTUMN

I Hope

If you are lucky enough to not understand addiction, then good for you. I hope you never have to. I hope you never see someone you love disappear before your eyes while standing right in front of you. I hope you never have to lie awake all night praying the phone doesn't ring, yet hoping that it does. I hope you never know the feeling of doing everything you thought was right, and still watch it go all wrong. I hope you never love an addict . . .

I hope you never know what it means to live afraid of yourself. To never trust yourself. To fight a raging war inside for your own mind every moment. To feel unwanted and unworthy. To *need* something that you know is destroying you, and to do anything for it. To trade your life, your soul, and still end up broken and alone. To give away everything and everyone you had. To have no answers. To always question. To have no choice, yet have to choose to fight your battle. I hope you never have to live as an addict . . .

CORMISHA G.

Cool Breeze

The cool breeze from the early morning grass,
The sun peeking at me like we're playing a game of hide and
seek.
The smell of fresh grass and dirt,
Hearing the clap of each foot hitting the trail.
The itchy straw on my head.
The softness of the hair as I ride the horse.
I will never forget this moment, because that was the best
memory
I have when my mom and dad were together.
I think little people know what a family feels like.
This memory has been forgotten about until today.
It's crazy the things forgotten, and why it would come up at a
time when
I never thought about it before.
Something powerful to hold onto, to keep in mind.

Adrienne T.

I Will Stand Tall Because...

I've gone through so much hell & back. This life I've been
living has its tough times & its rough times. But it all makes me
the strong woman I have become. I'm a better person today &
can give my advice to others & know that they take it seriously.
I no longer live in fear & I'm able to take on whatever life
throws my way. I'm a strong survivor & I'm leading a better life
& I continue to Stand Tall.

I see a beautiful lady.
I see a strong woman.
I see a survivor.
I see a warrior.
I see ME.

My Prayer

Ass backwards totally flipped upside down. Reversed and contorted but somehow still standing on solid ground. Completely empty, a shell of what I used to be. Just a façade that consumes me and replicated my body. Appearing as if it were me. I smile fake smiles and look so caring and true. Never in my life have I been so unsure. What am I supposed to do when I don't know who I am. No matter how hard I try it seems no one gives a damn. I've spent so many years doing anything to make others happy that I don't even know what it is that makes me, Me. When I look in the mirror it's not me I see. All I want in life is to give myself a fair chance at society. After all, why wouldn't I use the tools that are given to everybody. And the crazy part, it's free. So why do I have such a problem with my insecurities. I wish I could see what they see. That maybe I am worth more than just pretty. I want to feel like I have the strength to shine brightly. So bright I would never have to worry about the night. I am so done with this fight. I have wasted so much of myself that it gives me such a fright. God help me! I'm holding on with all my might, ever so tight, begging God please don't let me die tonight!

SHALANDA A.

My Life Has Made Me Strong

My life has made me strong
Struggles all day long
People tell me I'm doing it all wrong
Blissful ignorance was my favorite song
while I hit that bong
and played a game of beer pong.
Finally like someone hitting a gong
I realized all along
that I was being a ding dong—
and now I am learning to be strong!
And how to be right where before I was all wrong!

Delonna S.

Letter to My Four Children

I apologize for the chaos and mistakes I've made, and since I can't change what's already done I feel worthless, and I hide and constantly run as I face all the emotions and hurt I caused and chose not to see. I feel stronger and ready, 'cause it's all starting back with me. I hate that I hurt you. I hate that I changed. I don't know how to stop this spiral fueled by all the guilt and all this shame.

It's hard to admit and accept I'm not in control of my life, so I sit here empty inside as I watch my dreams fade at the end of the pipe. I can't remember when things in my world got turned upside down, but it seems like yesterday I was making you proud. I want so badly to be the mom you truly deserve, but I can't stand my reflection 'cause I know I'm not her.

I'm struggling to find my way back to when things were good. And I start every day with intentions to do right, and I wish that I could. I want you to know and believe my love for you never changed. My priorities and emotions just got so mixed up and rearranged. It's gonna take time to sort it all out, and it's not gonna be easy.

There are so many questions filled with doubt. We will all have to accept things will never be the same, but I'll never give up. I'll fight with all that I am each and every day. We've got to be humble and patient and not all expect right away. I've got to stay focused on "just for today."

I regret that I stole things from you that I'll never be able to replace, like the hope and trust I once saw as I looked at your beautiful faces. I know it seems like a cycle of lies that never ends. And I feel lost, but I'm in here—we just gotta find "me" again. I'm constantly wishing to take away your tears and your pain. So I'll seek guidance, and I'll continue to pray.

I'm looking forward to living better than the life we had, and to see you happy instead of betrayed and so sad. I miss you guys more than words could ever explain, so I'm going [to get help] to prove to you I'm finally ready to change.

I'm embarrassed of the lives I've told and the times you felt abandoned, alone and also mad. I've got a favor for you: please don't ever give up on me—and have faith that one day we won't be so sad.

And please please don't ever hate me for the life that you had!

STEPHANIE W.

Stand Tall: An Anaphora Poem

I will stand tall because…
  I am not a quitter
  I have a strong will
  and a soft heart.

I will stand tall because…
  I have what it takes
  to be the best mother,
  daughter, and wife
  that I can be.

I will stand tall because…
  nothing will get in
  my way and nobody
  can judge me for
  only what they can see.

I will stand tall because…
  I am who I am and
  I'll always be me from
  the end to the start.

I will always stand tall because
  I'm made not to fall.

Adrienne T.

I Remember

I remember one of the many houses I grew up in. There was a green apple tree & my mom would make fresh homemade apple pie.

I remember a white, barn-style shed in the backyard next to the apple tree, & it was padlocked & I somehow convinced by big brother Sean to unlock it. He did & I opened the boxes marked Christmas & threw the glass ornaments on the ground, cause I liked the sound they made. And one of the shards of glass struck my cheek. I now have a scar & a memory I can never forget.

I remember watching football with my dad down in the musty basement. He'd be in his favorite recliner (ugly as hell) & I'd be on the floor, which was yellow & brown shag carpeting. I'd have my coloring book & My Little Pony collection.

He'd get on the floor with me during commercials & color & play with me. I later had My Little Pony collection slowly disappear as we moved many times after my parents' divorce.

Anonymous

Will Someone Who Knows

Will someone who knows
Where all the time goes,
    Come take me away, by the hand . . .

I know day by day
    I've been fading away
And it's more than my heart can stand . . .

It's not like he knew
More than any men do
    But he knew all my heart ever had . . .

As winter grows near
All the free birds gather here
    Yet all of our songs sound so sad . . .

Lynette M

How Our Group Poem Made Me Feel

This poem made me feel proud, proud of my
peers & myself . . .
we all have so much to say, so many feelings
to express!
We are women with big, kind hearts.
It made me smile as well as tear up,
to be able to feel what others
feel in their hearts.
There is so much talent in one small place!
And we can all have a positive future
if we choose to rehabilitate!
I pray for everyone here
to be able to do what it takes
to feel less lonely.
I love you my sisters
who make me feel less lonely!

THE WRITE AGE—
GOLDEN PUBLIC LIBRARY

KIRSTEN MORGAN

Introduction
The Write Age—Golden Public Library

I approached the possibility of a Write Age group in Golden with a lot of questions and a certain amount of trepidation. Would enough people come to make it worthwhile? Would they stay? How might group members relate to each other in an informal and somewhat non-structured setting? Most of my questions were answered and concerns quelled on the first day, as 15 writers, from beginners to those more accomplished, poured through the door, delighted to have this opportunity to write and share with others of their ilk. In subsequent weeks, more people came, a few dropped out and we slowly created a rhythm and structure that worked well for all.

We agreed, since the emphasis would be on facilitation rather than instruction, that the primary focus would be on reading work written at home and receiving positive feedback. This format works very well, as writers of wildly varying backgrounds come together to share, sigh, cry and occasionally burst into howls of laughter. Since writing choices are self-determined, genres include novels, short stories, poetry, a children's book, memoir and even a script, all of which are greeted with equal enthusiasm. Many of our writers have joined Lighthouse and take classes there, but all have stayed with our group as a comfortable place to give first air to their writing.

The group shows no sign of slowing down and instead writers continue to explore unfamiliar genres, take risks, show vulnerability and trust each other with the gift of their deepest thoughts, as well as with hilarious commentary on life's pitfalls and peccadillos . Our weekly two-hour meeting isn't long enough, so most of us adjourn to a coffee shop after class to continue the conversation over lunch. Who could have guessed that this random group of writers, whose only common thread is being of "a certain age," would soon become each other's great friends, fans and relentless cheerleaders?

MICHAEL KEATING

Home

Today my daughter and I are going home. A brand-new house simply constructed by Habitat for Humanity and volunteers from all over the country. We will hang up our 4 black house numbers on to the front porch: 1229 Port Street. We will plant climbing star jasmine vines by the porch for the soft, light, otherworldly aroma.

We will plant a blood orange tree in our back yard to fill baskets with bright orange fruit for our table. We will put 2 chairs on the porch and say "howdee" to all our neighbors as they pass by. I will sip my cafe-au-lait in the morning before going to work and maybe sip a cold Dixie beer after work. This is now our home.

It was our time to go back to the lower 9th Ward. We had been staying at my brother's in Houston for these past 3 years. It was crowded, but this is kin. Over time this small 2-bedroom house became our home in Houston. It was christened with tears, laughter and sad memories. Now it is time to go home.

While in Houston I completed my GED while working labor construction for the Kinder Morgan Pipelines. I also had completed the first year of basic nursing credits at Houston Community College. I now have a 2-year grant at the University of Holy Cross Nursing School in New Orleans and intend to give back to my community when I graduate.

We have three suitcases and a box of food. My brother will be bringing what little furniture we have in his truck tomorrow but tonight we sleep at home even if it is just in a sleeping bag. We will be home tonight.

It is not the home that I grew up in and it is not neighborhood that I grew up in. But it is close. Three years ago, everything I knew, everything I loved, everything owned was taken away from me. My family. My home. My people. The storm broke everything and crushed my heart and my soul.

Three years ago, the category 4 storm headed towards us, I begged Memau, my Grandmother, to evacuate but she was sure the Lord would protect her. "My fate is in Jesus's hands. Amen"

"This nothing to do with god, we need to go now" I said. Memau said "our peoples comes from the original cadiens and I am 15 percent Choctaw Indian. Our family helped the runaway slaves, run out of Jim Crow and now I'm tired of runn'n. I still hope to celebrate those Choctaw Mardi Gras Indians every year at Mardi Gras". Her house was washed away. They never found her body. It was a sore that will never heal.

My mom had been recently living with a musician that hung out at Rip's Old 9th Ward Bar. I called and called to see if she was safe. She never picked up her cell. They identified her body a week later. My dad left years ago. Every now and then I would hear he was in town, but we never seen to connect. This is home. Every day we say a prayer to all those volunteers that helped us make this dream. This is home.

SAOIRSE CHARIS-GRAVES

Avatar

Perhaps he descended into this equine body
The embodiment of
Presence Of "Being With"

Perhaps he saw my need
My confusion
The cleaving of my soul

I could not claim a "Self"
She took it from me
Her need for an identity greater than her maternal duty

I could not voice a "need"
Too small, too big
And plainly, not her need so therefore not a need at all

I could not turn to him
Lying in the silver casket, eyes closed, body cold
He left me behind

No self allowed, no needs allowed
The deepest wound, wondering, wandering
In search of the one I am meant to be

Parome walks to me as soon as I enter the paddock
Brings his long face into mine
Warm breath from his nostril in my ear

"I am here," he says.
"I am here for you," he says.
"I will stay," he says.
And so he does.

Minutes into hours
He stands
Leaning his shoulder into my chest
As I stroke his neck, his face, his back

I bury my face in his neck
His skin quivers
My soul peeks out from the crevasse

Into which I have fallen
Long ago
He is more mother than I've ever known
More father than I was allowed.
With him, in his presence,
I may yet be whole.

MARY GATTUSO

a blip on the screen

reel to reel
modern musical
drama comedy
co-created
flash fiction
subtitles in Romance
subtleties in touch
co-starring
the Players
don't miss a cue
or a dead line
no edits or cuts
camera Obscura
low light
slow speed
steady
move in
a wrap
a love scene
a trap
a blip on the screen
caught between
two worlds
reel to real

MARCIE MILLER

Passport

For as long as I've had a passport, some thirty-five years now, I've gotten no small amount of enjoyment from looking at the stamps from all the places I've been. And whenever it's time to renew my passport, it's a matter of some relief to me that the expired one, stamped "Cancelled" is returned with the new one.

For without my old passports, I might not remember the beginnings and endings of my adventures in quite the same way. I can tell from my photo album that I've been to the Caribbean, but it's the stamp bearing the name "Dockyards of Antigua and Barbuda" that reminds me that I traveled from St. Thomas to Tortola on the "Bomba Charger." It was a sturdy vessel with a toothy shark's grin painted on the bow that plunged through the waves, occasionally drenching the passengers. Indeed, my carefully cultivated air of sophistication went quickly by the wayside when I took a rogue wave full in the face, much to the amusement of my fellow travelers. The ice was broken, and upon arriving on Tortola, several of my new friends treated me to cool Red Stripe beer and games of pool on tattered felt while we waited at the dockyard to board the "Flying Cloud," a very different kind of vessel.

I also particularly like the stamp from Monserrat – it's in the shape of a cloverleaf because that Caribbean island was once Irish territory. I think it's especially fitting that they use green ink.

Many years ago, when I traveled to Poland and the Czech Republic just after Vaclav Havel's Velvet Revolution, I received several new stamps. My arrival in Warsaw by plane was noted on August 19; the stamp has a tiny jet on it. Then, when I crossed the border by rail at Zhebzedovice, the stamp has a cute little train. I have lots of little train stamps because you get one on either side of the border – one on the Polish side and one on the Czech side, and I liked Prague so much, I kept going back.

Prague is a beautiful, magical place, and not easily forgettable, but were it not for all the little train stamps, I might not remember that three of my four trips between Prague and Krakow were on the night train, and one was alone. Being jolted awake periodically by conductors and border patrol guards who shout unintelligible things in a language not my own convinced me that the day train might be more to my liking.

Perhaps it was being in a former Eastern Bloc country, perhaps it was the uniforms, or the language, or the shouting, but I imagined what it could have been like for many who fled the Iron Curtain. So, I'm glad I took the night train, and I'm glad I did it once by myself. It scared the hell out of me and it made me feel brave. On my last trip to Prague, however, my brand new passport was scanned by a computer in Denver, and never taken out again until my arrival in that cobbled city. No one at Kennedy International even asked about it. I was relieved when I got the little jet stamp in Prague.

Now, anyone who knows me knows I love computers. I love their power and the elegant way they handle information. But I'm not sure I want a computer to keep track of my travels. I don't think I like having my comings and goings reduced to so many bits and bytes on the information super highway. It's too cold, too analytical. What I want is a stamp! They can scan my passport if they want, and let the computer remember my travels, but stamp it too, please, so I can remember my adventures!

Linda Schwab Messmer

Inspiration

I'm new to this writing thing
  And maybe haven't found my groove
  But it surprises me how quickly
  It's become a part of me, a necessity even, as ideas and emotions
flow and I want to express them some way, somehow.
  But the writing down, the process, the following of a path I
didn't know was there . . .
  It's hard to find the words that will resonate with others . . . and
this is how I try . . .
  The first place I think of when pondering the perfect setting
to inspire my most magical, deep thoughts would be to sit in the
middle of a Rocky Mountain forest, with nothing but wildlife and
endless miles of pines and aspen surrounding me. Because I've
always wanted to be a tree. Tall, silent, stable, enduring . . .
  A knowing observer of day and night, the changing seasons, of
deer and elk, squirrels, chipmunks, raccoons, porcupines, going
about their life beneath me, unafraid of human intruders and
scampering through my limbs. Holding birds in my arms, watching over a nest and fledgling babies.
  Even experiencing the fury of a wildfire up close . . . when a
tree burns, does it hurt?
  But realistically, writing in a forest, after sitting on the ground

very long, my butt would hurt.

My back and aching joints would remind me of my age as I slowly, with difficulty stand back up. Besides, there are crawling ticks, the weather might change, and I would be too hot or too cold.

I might be drenched in a sudden thunderstorm or even struck by lightning.

So . . . I also think of writing near Harriman Lake, one of my favorite walking spots.

Sitting on a lovely comfortable bench, I am inspired by the birds – red-winged blackbirds, mallards, cormorants, red-tailed hawks, owls, white pelicans, and even an occasional eagle.

Because if I couldn't be a tree, I've always wanted to be a bird.

Flying, floating above the earth, must be the most freeing feeling of all.

I would have a new perspective from far above, away from traffic and earthly turmoil and I would understand bird-speak. I would send messages of warning, wooing, and planning for the trip south to my friends and family and sometimes sing just for the joy of it.

But then, the bugs are REALLY bad at Harriman. I would have to wear stinky bug spray and even then, the nasty little gnats get in your eyes, ears, and nose if you sit still very long. And if you're too close to the lakeshore, chances are good there's a rotting dead fish nearby or gross-looking bait, or hooks and fishing line to trip on, left by the many fishermen. And there's hardly any shade at all at Harriman Lake.

My next choice is to sit by a running stream, or creek or river because the water always brings me peace. The alternate churning, rough spots, and fleeting calm...ever moving forward no matter what...seem more than just a metaphor to me. I FEEL my soul in the cold mountain streams. And if I become really still, if I listen really carefully and I stare really hard, my life – past, present and future – are crystal clear in the water below me.

But again, sitting on rocks no longer works for me. That hurts even more than sitting in the dirt. And I either have to drive a long distance to find a quiet spot or I face a crowd of other people, swimming, fishing, picnicking and enjoying the beauty of the water too…but they interrupt my thoughts.

A practical option is my back patio – it's beautiful and close at hand…I have written out there occasionally. It's quiet and peaceful, and in June and July wild explosions of pink roses cover the trellis, little birds busily build nests, landing near me with grass in their mouths, cute bunnies everywhere, just enough huge trees to give privacy and shade.

Our growing garden getting closer to harvest brings inspiration and appreciation of the life cycle of the flowers and vegetables we planted from tiny seeds. This should spark something very profound.

I even play my favorite music to set the mood – it depends, I might listen to Vivaldi, Spanish guitar, Led Zeppelin or the Beatles, heavy metal, or…like my sweet 13-year-old granddaughter told me the other day, her current music of choice is "rap with cuss words" – yes sometimes that works for me too.

Since I'm at home, I can easily set up the many essentials for thoughtful writing on the patio, including my laptop, the power cord, my mouse and mousepad, my reading glasses, my sunglasses, pen and paper, my cellphone, my grande iced sugar-free vanilla latte from Starbucks, and 4 or 5 pillows placed exactly right in my chair so my back doesn't hurt.

Then the sun moves and I have to adjust the umbrella. The music on Pandora is wonderful at first but a song comes on that I just can't tolerate and I have to quickly hit Thumbs Down so it will STOP! I notice that the roses need trimming, the beans have all been eaten by the rabbits - and then squawking magpies and bluejays arrive to terrorize the baby birds, not hidden well enough in our trees. I run for a broom to chase them off and try to guard my little bird families, knowing those predators will probably win as soon as I turn my back.

All the while, it takes all my energy to block the knowledge that yes, my surroundings are profound – profoundly EMPTY. Until recently, my sweet dog filled every inch of the yard, the grass, the garden, the patio, her fur brushing against my legs. The real reason those damn rabbits are eating all the beans is because she isn't here to eat the beans this year. She's missing from the picture now and I can't write about her yet. I wonder if the neighbors can hear me stifling my sobs.

It was a TERRIBLE idea to write out here. I am no longer in the mood.

For now, I'm finding my inspiration comes unexpectedly…Since I retired, I'm more aware of that insistent internal voice, repeating old events, past hurts and mistakes, moments of great happiness, worrying and pondering the future—the stories are seemingly unstoppable. Thoughts are more vivid now and no longer side-tracked by my work. It feels like the emotions and words MUST spill out of my brain and onto paper or laptop and I write at any time I feel driven.

It might be when I wake up in the morning, and in my very first moments of alertness, just the right words occur to me to use in a certain phrase. In the shower, I turn an idea over and over until it dawns on me that the subject I thought I wanted to explore is really something else entirely. As I get into bed at night, I sometimes hop back out and jot down the perfect word to insert in a verse, so I don't forget it by tomorrow. The impulse to write happens when my two sons send me a group text and it makes me laugh out loud, a joke or a memory that only the three of us understand. . . . I want to share that feeling of joy with the world.

I want to capture my ongoing discovery of my husband's personality and heart. We've been married a whole 8 years now and I'm finally growing to understand spousal love, accepting that even though we can irritate each other to the core, we also care about and care for each other to the core.

He cracks a ridiculous joke or smiles at me and I'm taken aback at how much he matters to me.

How can I put that into words without sounding sappy or mimicking more eloquent writers before me about feelings that are so common and obvious to others but are brand new to me?

Writing has me thinking differently now when I have lunch with a friend, and she articulates brilliantly an experience or a concept that I could never put into words before, even though once she says it, I feel like I've always known it. As soon as I get home, I open my laptop to add that new topic to my list or use it to rework a piece already in progress. And the same happens tenfold when I sit spellbound in a group of savvy writers on Mondays in the Golden Library.

It seems these days that inspiration comes from every direction—memories are more powerful, my surroundings are more brilliant, every conversation more meaningful. Knowing I want to capture what I see, think, and feel, I pay more attention. I find that I am thankful for a deadline and an audience. I write hit and miss, and I love it.

ANDREW D. MELICK

Saturday Morning

A song named "Come Saturday Morning" debuted in late 1969. The theme of a movie, starring Liza Minelli, about an adolescent love affair that ends in heartache. Both the song and Liza were nominated for Academy awards. The song fared well on the "Easy Listening" charts, but it also lasted several weeks on the Billboard Top Forty. I must have first heard it on the kitchen radio, which was usually tuned to a local AM station that played the latest hits. The emotional power of music had just begun to infiltrate my 11-year-old consciousness, and with its wistful melody and plaintive lyrics, "Come Saturday Morning" found my soft spot.

My exposure to popular music back then also came through my oldest brother, who was 17 and with whom I often listened to 45s on his record player. But he never would have had "Come Saturday Morning" in his collection. Way too sweet and sentimental for his tastes. He was into loud, raucous rock and roll, music with a good beat.

I, on the other hand, was a sucker for sappy songs. Maybe I was born to have my heart broken. Or maybe my heart always was broken, and I have forever been putting it back together. Regardless, it was love songs and sad songs which drew me to them the most. Songs that evoked a yearning for something just beyond my reach, or songs that plumbed a bottomless sorrow at my very core. Songs like that made me want to cry.

My musical preferences were no doubt determined by my emotional nature. I was a touchy kid, growing up. It did not take much to make me cry, and I cried a lot. At least that is the way I remember it.

Then again, it could be I cried no more than any other kid my age; perhaps it only seemed that way because every time I did cry, I felt overwhelmingly ashamed of myself. Somewhere along the line, obviously early on, I got the message that crying was for sissies, that emotional vulnerability was a weakness. The agony of fighting back the tears, rather than their frequency, could very well be what is stamped on my memory.

I recall one day in kindergarten when something happened that hurt my feelings. I knew I was going to cry, so I hid behind the piano, out of sight. And it worked! If the teacher knew I was crying, or if any of the other kids knew, no one ever let on. I had kept my weakness a secret, a monumental victory.

I continued to repress my perceived hypersensitivity, and with practice, I got better at it. One of the last times I cried was when my first girlfriend broke up with me. We were both 16. She was the person from whom I first heard the words, "I love you," and until the moment those words were withdrawn, which was the only way I could interpret the fact that she wanted to date other guys, I never fully grasped just how important that statement was, or how much it had changed my life.

I had a newly minted junior driver's license, and I was dropping her off at her house when she let the bomb fall. I never saw it coming and melted into a miserable pile of tears. She cried too, but that did little to relieve my humiliation. She had seen the real me, the crybaby. On the drive home, "Come Saturday Morning" played on the car radio. I sobbed so uncontrollably I had to stop on the side of the road.

I managed to pull myself together, however, and I got through the next day at school as if it was no big deal. Within a couple of weeks, I was dating another girl, one of a long string of superficial relationships, women to whom I never got too close, and certainly never allowed to get too close to me. So went my transition from emotional to emotion-less.

The author Pat Conroy wrote that the souls of men wither for the most obvious reason: their faces are not adequately watered. The toll of stoicism, especially as it is practiced by men in many modern cultures, is well-documented and nothing new. My own example is just one among millions. I have saved myself a lot of emotional pain, no doubt, but at what cost? I have missed countless opportunities to experience the joy of giving love, the finest emotion we can know. All on account of the monumental fear of being revealed for what I truly am: a tender-hearted man whose feelings sometimes get hurt.

I also know, however, that the vulnerable part of me has never been fully vanquished, and deep down, I still cherish its existence. Perhaps I even love that part of me best. When I was old enough to start collecting a paycheck, my first major purchase was a hi-fi stereo system. With the money that remained, I started buying LPs. I would lie for hours on my bedroom floor, positioned perfectly between the speakers, floating in the ethereal world of music: an invisible and intangible world of pure emotion. An infinite world, and yet the nearest world there is.

Through the years, when it feels safe—when I am alone, with eyes closed—I have occasionally embraced feelings of love and hope and sadness, none of which I can define, and which often overlap. It has probably been decades since I devoted any time to listening to music for its own sake, with no other distraction. Yet even today, if I happen to hear a song such as "Come Saturday Morning," I can still be transported to the mysterious realm of human sentiment and lose myself there. Sometimes, if no one is looking, I even start to cry.

Dan Manzanares, Community Programs Coordinator

Acknowledgments

Lighthouse Writers Workshop would like to thank the following people without whom our community engagement programs could not be possible: Stacey Grijalva from Denver Public Library; Simone Groene-Nieto, Cecilia LaFrance, and Tana Lucero from Jefferson County Public Library; Meghan Frank and Steve Hartbauer from The Gathering Place; Lena Carillo and Lilly Cervantes from A Colorado Women's Correctional Facility; Sarah Ford from the Denver VOICE; Sarah El Hage and Jessie Durham from Veterans Affairs; Rolf Stavig from UC Health, and Lisa A. Trigilio and James Ginsburg from the Fort Lyon Supportive Residential Community.

Unending thanks to the Lighthouse faculty and staff, facilitators, and volunteers for their intelligence, compassion, and dedication to not only the Lighthouse outreach mission but to the writers as well. Thank you Kathy Conde, Gay Porter DeNileon, Susanna Donato, Alex Donovan, Wren Duggan, Laurie Duncan, Sierra Fleenor, Darcee Freier, Susan Friberg, Michael J. Henry, Joyce Hoverter, John Holley, Alice Johnson, Connie Klein, Ray Kemble, Danielle Krolewicz, Kelsi Long, Mell McDonnell, Rudy Melena, Courtney E. Morgan, Kirsten Morgan, Dani Rado, Marlene Rezvani, Joy Roulier Sawyer, Scotty Sawyer, Kat Svaldi, Annette Taylor, Jane Thatcher, Seth Brady Tucker, Denise Gonzalez-Walker, Heather Wood, Hana Zittel, and Connie Zumpf.

Please join us in thanking all the organizations and individuals who made this book possible.

Art Works (National Endowment for the Arts)

Colorado Creative Industries

Community First Foundation

Denver Arts & Venues

Denver Public Library: Central & Decker Branches

Jefferson County Public Library: Libary 2 You and the Arvada & Golden Branches

McWethy Charitable Fund

SCFD of Denver and Jefferson Counties

Stranahan Foundation

A Colorado Women's Correctional Facility

Denver VOICE Writing Workshop

Fort Lyon Writer-in-Residence Program

The Gathering Place Writers' Group

UC Health Creative Writing Workshop

Veterans Affairs Writing Workshop

Along with the generosity of many individual donors

Made in the USA
Columbia, SC
24 March 2019